C0042 36802

THE VAGRANT MOOD

William Somerset Maugham was born in 1874 and lived in Paris until he was ten. He was educated at King's School, Canterbury, and at Heidelberg University. He spent some time at St. Thomas's Hospital with the idea of practising medicine, but the success of his first novel, *Liza of Lambeth*, published in 1897, won him over to letters. *Of Human Bondage*, the first of his masterpieces, came out in 1915, and with the publication in 1919 of *The Moon and Sixpence* his reputation as a novelist was established. His position as a successful playwright was being consolidated at the same time. His first play, *A Man of Honour*, was followed by a series of successes just before and after World War I, and his career in the theatre did not end until 1933 with *Sheppey*.

His fame as a short story writer began with *The Trembling of a Leaf*, subtitled *Little Stories of the South Sea Islands*, in 1921, after which he published more than ten collections. His other works include travel books such as *On a Chinese Screen* and *Don Fernando*, essays, criticism, and the autobiographical *The Summing Up* and *A Writer's Notebook*.

In 1927 Somerset Maugham settled in the South of France and lived there until his death in 1965.

D1355483

ALSO BY W. SOMERSET MAUGHAM

W. Somerset Maugham

THE VAGRANT MOOD

V

VINTAGE

Published by Vintage 2001

2 4 6 8 10 9 7 5 3 1

Copyright © The Royal Literary Fund

This book is sold subject to the condition that it shall not
by way of trade or otherwise, be lent, resold, hired out, or
otherwise circulated without the publisher's prior consent in
any form of binding or cover other than that in which it is
published and without a similar condition including this
condition being imposed on the subsequent purchaser

First published in Great Britain in 1952
by William Heinemann

Vintage
Random House, 20 Vauxhall Bridge Road,
London SW1V 2SA

Random House Australia (Pty) Limited
20 Alfred Street, Milsons Point, Sydney
New South Wales 2061, Australia

Random House New Zealand Limited
18 Poland Road, Glenfield,
Auckland 10, New Zealand

Random House (Pty) Limited
Endulini, 5A Jubilee Road, Parktown 2193,
South Africa

The Random House Group Limited Reg. No. 954009
www.randomhouse.co.uk

A CIP catalogue record for this book
is available from the British Library

ISBN 0 09 928679 3

Papers used by Random House are natural, recyclable
products made from wood grown in sustainable forests.
The manufacturing processes conform to the environ-
mental regulations of the country of origin

Glasgow City Council
Cultural & Leisure Services
Libraries Info. & Learning

L		
C 00423589		
Askews		17-Jun-2009
824.912 *LT*		£7.99

Contents

Three of the essays in this volume appeared in *The Cornhill*. One was delivered as a lecture at the Philosophical Colloquium of the University of Columbia, but I have rewritten it in the hope of making it more easily readable. Part of the final essay appeared many years ago in *Life and Letters*.

W. S. M.

Augustus

I

I think I must be one of the few persons still alive who knew Augustus Hare. I had published a first novel which had had some success and he asked a common friend, a minor canon of St. Paul's, to invite me to dinner so that we might meet. I was young, twenty-four, and shy; but he took a fancy to me, because, tongue-tied though I was, I was content to listen while he discoursed, and shortly afterwards he wrote to me from Holmhurst, his house in the country, and asked me to come down for the week-end. I became a frequent guest.

Since the kind of life he lived there is lived no longer, I think it may be not without interest to describe the daily round. Sharp at eight in the morning a maid in a rustling print dress and a cap with streamers came into your room with a cup of tea and two slices of thin bread and butter, which she placed on the night table; if it was winter a tweeny followed her, in a print dress too, but not so shiny nor so rustling, who raked out the ashes of the fire which had been lit the night before, and laid and lit another. At half-past eight the maid came in again with a small can of hot water. She emptied the basin in which you had made a pretence of washing before going to bed, put the can in the basin and covered it with a towel. While she was thus occupied the tweeny brought in a sitz-bath, laid a white mat so that water should not splash the carpet, and on it, in front of the blazing fire, placed the sitz-bath. On each side of this she set a large can of hot water and a large can of cold, the soap-dish from the washing-stand

and a bath-towel. The maids retired. The sitz-bath must be unknown to the present generation. It was a round tub perhaps three feet in diameter, about eighteen inches deep, with a back that rose to your shoulder-blades when you were sitting in it. Outside it was japanned a bilious yellow and inside painted white. As there was no room for your legs, they dangled outside, and you had to be something of a contortionist to wash your feet. You could do nothing about your back but trickle water down it from your sponge. The advantage of the contraption was that as your legs and back were out of the water you had no occasion to dawdle as you do in a bath in which you can lie full length, so that though you lost the happy thoughts and fruitful reflections which you might otherwise have had, you were ready to go downstairs at nine o'clock when the breakfast bell rang.

Augustus was already in his chair at the head of the table, laid for the hearty meal he was soon to partake of. In front of him was the great family Bible and a large Prayer Book bound in black leather. Seated, he looked solemn and even imposing. Standing, however, because he had a long body and short legs, he lost something of his impressiveness and indeed looked a trifle ridiculous. The guests took their seats and the servants trooped in. A row of chairs had been placed for them in front of the sideboard, on which, besides a noble ham and a brace of cold pheasants, various good things to eat were kept hot in silver entrée dishes by the thin blue flames of methylated spirit. Augustus read a prayer. He had a strident, somewhat metallic voice and he read in a tone that seemed to suggest that he was not one to stand any nonsense from the deity. Sometimes it happened that a guest was a minute or two late; he opened the door very cautiously and slunk in on tiptoe, with the air of one who seeks to make himself invisible. Augustus did not look up; he paused in the middle of a sentence and remained silent till the late-comer had seated himself, and then proceeded from where he had left off. The air was heavy with reproof. But that was all: Augustus made no reference afterwards to the sluggard's tardiness. When he had read a certain number of prayers Augustus closed the book and opened the Bible. He read the passages marked for the day, and having finished, uttered the words: 'Let us pray.' This was the signal for us all to kneel, the guests on hassocks and the servants on the Turkey carpet, and we recited in chorus the Lord's Prayer. Then we scrambled to our feet, the cook and the maids scuttled out of the room; in a moment the parlour-maid brought in tea and coffee, removed Bible and Prayer Book, and put the tea-kettle and coffee-pot in their place.

I was accustomed to family prayers and I noticed that some of the prayers Augustus read sounded strangely in my ears. Then I discovered that he had neatly inked out many lines in the Prayer Book he read from. I asked him why.

'I've crossed out all the passages in glorification of God,' he said. 'God is certainly a gentleman, and no gentleman cares to be praised to his face. It is tactless, impertinent and vulgar. I think all that fulsome adulation must be highly offensive to him.'

At the time this notion seemed odd to me and even comic, but since then I have come to think that there was some sense in it.

After breakfast Augustus retired to his study to write the autobiography on which he was then engaged. He neither smoked himself, nor allowed smoking in the house, so that such of his guests as hankered for the first pipe of the day had to go out of doors, which was pleasant enough in summer when you could sit down with a book in the garden, but not so pleasant in winter when you had to seek shelter in the stables.

Luncheon, a substantial meal of eggs or macaroni, joint, if there were no left-overs from the night before, with vegetables and a sweet, was at one; and after a decent

3

interval Augustus, in a dark town suit, black boots, a stiff collar and a bowler hat, took his guests for a walk in the grounds. The property was small, rather less than forty acres, but by planning and planting he had given it something of the air of a park in a great country house. As you walked along he pointed out the improvements he had made, the resemblance he had achieved here to the garden of a Tuscan villa, the spacious view he had contrived there, and the wooded walks he had designed. I could not but observe that notwithstanding his objection to treating God with fulsome adulation, he accepted the compliments of his guests with a good deal of complacency. The promenade ended with a visit to the Hospice. This was a cottage he had arranged for the entertainment of gentle-women in reduced circumstances. He invited them for a month at a time, supplied them with their travelling expenses, farm and garden produce and groceries. He enquired if they were comfortable and had everything they wanted. No duchess, bringing calves-foot jelly and half a pound of tea to a cottager on the estate, could have combined condescension with beneficence with a more delicate sense of the difference that exists between the conferring of favours and the accepting of them.

After that it was time to go back to tea. This was a copious repast of scones, muffins or crumpets, bread and butter, jam, plain cake and currant cake. The better part of an hour was spent over this, and Augustus talked of his early life, his travels and his many friends. At six he went to his study to write letters and we met again when the second bell called us down to dinner. We were waited on by maids in black uniforms, white caps and aprons, and were given soup, fish, poultry or game, sweet and savoury; sherry with the soup and fish, claret with the game, and port with the nuts and fruit. After dinner we returned to the drawing-room. Sometimes Augustus read aloud to us, sometimes we played an intolerably tedious game called Halma, or, if he thought the company worthy, he told us his famous stories. The clock struck ten and Augustus rose from his chair by the fire. We marched out into the hall, where candles in silver candle-sticks were waiting for us, lit them and walked upstairs to our respective bedrooms. There was a can of hot water in the basin and a fire blazed in the hearth. It was difficult to read by the light of a single candle, but it was enchanting to lie in a four-poster and watch the glow of the fire till the sleep of youth descended upon you.

Such was a day in one of the smaller country houses at the end of the nineteenth century, and such, more or less, throughout the land was the day in hundreds upon hundreds of houses belonging to persons who, without being rich, were well enough off to live in the great comfort which they looked upon as the way in which gentlefolk should live. Augustus was houseproud, and nothing pleased him more than to show guests the relics of a 'wealthy past', with which Holmhurst was filled. It was a rambling house of no architectural merit, with wide corridors and low ceilings, but by adding another room or two, building archways in the garden, decorating it here and there with urns and statues, among which was one of Queen Anne and her four satellites which had once stood in front of St. Paul's, Augustus had managed to give the place an air. It might have been the dower-house on the estate of a great nobleman, which, if there was no dowager to inhabit it, might be appropriately lent to an aunt who was the relict of a former ambassador to the Ottoman court.

II

Augustus was profoundly conscious of the fact that he was the representative of an ancient county family, the Hares of Hurstmonceux, connected, though distantly, with members of the aristocracy; and though its fortunes were fallen, his sense of the consequence this gave him remained unabated. He was like an exiled king, surrounded with such objects of departed grandeur as he has saved from the wreck, who is hail-fellow-well-met with the rag-tag and bobtail his altered circumstances force him to frequent, but who is alert to watch for the bobs and bows that his graciousness might induce ill-conditioned persons to omit.

Though Augustus was apt to mention with a deprecating smile that he was descended from a younger son of King Edward I, the family fortunes were founded by Francis Hare, a clever parson who had the good luck to be Sir Robert Walpole's tutor at King's College, Cambridge. Walpole's advancement, as we know, was furthered by Sarah, Duchess of Marlborough, and it may be surmised that it was by her influence that Francis Hare was appointed Chaplain-General to the forces in the Low Countries. He rode by the side of the great general at the battles of Blenheim and Ramillies. With such powerful friends it is not surprising that his merits did not go unrewarded. He was made Dean of Worcester and then of St. Paul's; and the second of these lucrative offices he continued to hold when he was created first Bishop of St. Asaph's and then Bishop of Chichester. He made two very profitable marriages. By his first wife, Bethaia Naylor, he had a son, Francis, who inherited the vast and romantic castle of Hurstmonceux and a handsome estate, and then added the name of Naylor to that of Hare. By his second wife, a great heiress, he had a son Robert, whose godfather, Sir Robert Walpole, as a christening present bestowed on him the sinecure office of sweepership of Gravesend, worth £400 a year. This he held to the day of his death. Sir Robert took sufficient interest in his old tutor's son to advise that he should adopt the Church as his profession, since he could thus best provide for his future. Robert took orders and was given first a living and then a canonry at Winchester. The bishop was a prudent man and while Robert was still very young arranged a marriage for him with the heiress of a property close to that of his own wife. By her he had two sons, Francis and Robert, and soon after her death he married another heiress. His elder brother died childless and the Canon of Winchester inherited Hurstmonceux Castle. The bishop must have been well satisfied with his son's station in life.

The bishop's descendants, however, seem to have inherited little of his worldly wisdom, for from that time the fortunes of the family began to decline. The first step was taken by the canon's second wife. She dismantled the castle and from it took the floors, doors and chimney-pieces for a large new house called Hurstmonceux Place which she built in another part of the park. The canon's eldest son, Francis Hare-Naylor, the grandfather of our Augustus, was a good-looking ne'er-do-well, bold, witty and extravagant; he seems to have got himself periodically arrested for debt and in order to extricate himself from his difficulties was obliged to raise money on his prospects from the Hurstmonceux estates. He had taken the fancy of Georgiana, Duchess of Devonshire, who introduced him to her cousin Georgiana, daughter of Jonathan Shipley, Bishop of St. Asaph. The pair eloped, whereupon their respective families 'renounced them with fury' and neither the Bishop of St. Asaph nor the Canon of Winchester ever saw them again. They went abroad and lived on the two hundred pounds a year which the Duchess allowed them. They had four sons, Francis, Augustus, Julius and Marcus. When Francis Hare-Naylor, the husband of Georgiana Shipley, eventually succeeded his father he sold the remnants of his ancestral estates for sixty thousand pounds. On his death, in 1815, his eldest son Francis Hare, for since he no longer owned Hurstmonceux he abandoned the additional name of Naylor, came into possession of what remained of the family fortunes, and

7

proceeded to live a life of pleasure till his circumstances obliged him, like many another spendthrift at that time, to take up his residence on the Continent. But he was apparently still well enough off to give large dinner parties twice a week. He kept good company and counted Count D'Orsay and Lady Blessington, Lord Desart, Lord Bristol, Lord Dudley among his more intimate friends. In 1828 he married Anne, a daughter of Sir John Paul, the banker, and by her had a daughter and three sons. The youngest of these, born in 1834, was the Augustus who is the subject of this essay.

Though the Hurstmonceux estates had been sold the family had retained the advowson of the rich living. The incumbent was the Reverend Robert Hare, the younger son of Francis Hare-Naylor, and it was understood that he should be succeeded by the Reverend Augustus Hare, one of Francis Hare's three brothers. Of Marcus, the youngest of the three, I have been able to discover nothing except that he married a daughter of Lord Stanley of Alderley, had a 'place' at Torquay, complained when he was staying at Hurstmonceux Rectory that the water with which the tea was made was never on the boil, and died in 1845. Julius was a Fellow of Trinity and a very learned man. With his brother Augustus he was the author of a book called *Guesses at Truth*, which in its day was popular with the devout. When the Reverend Robert Hare died his nephew the Reverend Augustus Hare did not wish to leave the parish of Alton Barnes, to which he had been appointed, and persuaded his brother Julius to accept the living of Hurstmonceux in his place. It was a wrench to Julius to leave Cambridge, but he had too great a sense of duty to allow a valuable piece of property to go out of the family and so consented to the sacrifice. He eventually became Archdeacon of Lewes.

The Reverend Augustus Hare married Maria, daughter of the Reverend Oswald Leicester, Rector of Stoke-upon-Terne. He died in Rome, whither he had gone for his health, in 1834, the year in which our Augustus was born. It was after him that my hero was named and the widow, Mrs. Augustus Hare, was his godmother. Francis and Anne Hare, the child's parents, found it none too easy to live in the style suitable to their position and at the same time support a family, and they were very much annoyed when their last son was born. Maria Hare was childless, and on her return to England after burying her husband it occurred to her that they might be willing to let her adopt her godson. She wrote to her sister-in-law and shortly afterwards received from her the following letter:

'My dear Maria, how very kind of you. Yes, certainly the baby shall be sent as soon as it is weaned; if anyone else would like one, would you kindly remember that we have others.'

The child in due course was 'sent over to England with a little green carpet-bag containing two little white night-shirts and a red coral necklace.'

Maria Hare's father, the Reverend Oswald Leicester, belonged to a family of great antiquity, which claimed direct descent from Gunnora, Duchess of Normandy, grandmother of William the Conqueror. He belonged thus to the same class as the Bertrams of Mansfield Park and Mr. Darcy of Pemberley. The Reverend Oswald Leicester was a sincere Christian, but he had a very proper notion of what befitted an English gentleman. He would have agreed with Lady Catherine de Bourgh that Elizabeth Bennet was not the sort of person Mr. Darcy should marry. Reginald Heber, the hymn-writer, afterwards Bishop of Calcutta, was Rector of Hodnet, which was only two miles from Maria Leicester's home, and she spent long periods with him and his wife. Reginald Heber had a curate called Martin Stow and since we are told nothing about his antecedents we must conclude that he was not 'a gentleman born'. Maria Leicester and Martin Stow fell in love with one another, but her father would not hear of his daughter's union with 'a mere country curate', and she was too dutiful a daughter to marry without his consent. When Reginald Heber was appointed to the bishopric of Calcutta he offered his Indian chaplaincy to Martin Stow, who accepted it in the hope that this preferment would induce the Reverend Oswald Leicester to look upon his suit with favour. His hope was frustrated, Maria and Martin met and parted, and a few months later the sad news was brought her that Mr. Stow had died of fever. Now, the Reverend Augustus Hare was a cousin of Mrs. Heber's and a friend of Martin Stow. He was the confidant of the lovers. His was a willing ear when they needed to pour out their troubles. On hearing of Martin Stow's death Maria Leicester wrote to Augustus Hare as follows:

'I must write a few lines, although I feel it almost needless to do so, for Augustus Hare knows all my feelings too well to doubt what they must be now ... it is to you I turn as the sharer, the fellow sufferer in my grief ... I know that if you can you will come here. When we have once met it will be a comfort to mourn together.'

They met, they corresponded, and, as Maria wrote in her Journal, 'unconsciously and imperceptibly the feelings of esteem and friendship,' with which she had regarded Augustus, 'assumed a new character, and something of the tenderness and beauty attending a warmer interest' took their place. Two years after the death of Martin Stow Augustus asked her to marry him and she agreed. 'Secure in the affection of Augustus,' she wrote again in her Journal, 'I feel no longer a blank in life, and everything takes a new and bright colouring.' But it was not till a year later that she received her father's consent to the engagement. It may be surmised that he gave it because he thought it would be for the happiness of his daughter, thirty-one years old by this time, an age then at which a maiden, as Mr. Wordsworth somewhat ungallantly put it, was withering on the stalk; but also because he thought an alliance between the Hares of Hurstmonceux, descended from a younger son of King Edward I, and the Leicesters of Toft, descended from Gunnora, Duchess of Normandy, could not but be regarded as suitable. Moreover, with the rich living of Hurstmonceux to fall to Augustus on the death of his Uncle Robert, Maria would be able to live in the style appropriate to a gentleman's daughter. Though both families were sincerely imbued with the conviction that this life was merely a post-inn, as it were, in which they sojourned for a brief space on their way to their heavenly home, they saw no reason why they should not make their temporary abode as comfortable as possible.

After the death of her husband Maria Hare spent some months with Julius, her brother-in-law, at Hurstmonceux and then took a house near-by, called Lime, which remained her home for twenty-five years. When she adopted the little Augustus, her godson, it was with the idea that he should be brought up to take Holy Orders and in due course succeed his Uncle Julius as Rector of Hurstmonceux. She started to train him in virtue from the beginning. When he was only eighteen months old she wrote in her Journal: 'Augustus has grown much more obedient, and is ready to give his food and playthings to others.' His religious education was her constant care and when he was three, by which time he could read and was learning German, she took pains to explain to him the mystery of the Trinity. When he was four his playthings were taken away from him and banished to the loft, so that he should learn that there were more serious things in life than toys. He had no companions of his own age. There was a poor woman who lived close to the gate of Lime whom Maria Hare often visited to relieve her necessities and by her pious exhortations persuade her to accept her lot as a special blessing of Providence. This woman had a little boy, whom Augustus longed to play with, and once did in a hayfield, but he was so severely punished for it that he never did again. To Mrs. Hare (Miss Leicester of Toft as was) it was not only a duty, it was a labour of love to visit the poor, but it was out of the question to allow a gentleman's son to play with a working-man's.

On March 13, 1839, she wrote in her Journal: 'My little Augustus is now five years old. Strong personal identity, reference of everything to himself, greediness of pleasure and possession, are I fear prominent features in his disposition. May I be taught how best to correct his sinful propensities with judgment, and to draw him out of self to live for others.'

Notwithstanding everything, however, Augustus was sometimes naughty. Then he was sent upstairs 'to prepare', which, I take it, means to take down his knicker-bockers and bare his little bottom, and Uncle Julius was bidden to come from his rectory to beat him. This he did with a riding-whip. Mrs. Hare was afraid of over-indulging the child and he only had to express a wish to have it refused. On one occasion she took him to visit the curate's wife and someone gave him a lollypop, which he ate, but when they got home the smell of peppermint betrayed him and he was given a large dose of rhubarb and soda with a forcing spoon to teach him in future to avoid carnal indulgence.

Meanwhile Maria Hare had made the acquaintance of the Misses Maurice, Priscilla and Esther, sisters of Frederick Maurice, the evangelist. They kept a school at Reading, but every year came to stay at Lime for a period. They were intensely, even aggressively, religious and they acquired a great influence over Mrs. Hare. One of its results was that she adopted more stringent measures so to form the character of Augustus that he might become a worthy minister of Christ. Till then he had had roast mutton and rice pudding every day for dinner. An occasion came when he was told that a delicious pudding was to be served. It was talked of till his mouth watered. It was placed on the table and he was just about to eat the helping he had been given when it was snatched away from him and he was told to get up and take it to some poor person in the village. Mrs. Hare wrote in her Journal: 'Augustus would, I believe, always do a thing if *reasoned* with about it, but the necessity of obedience without reasoning is especially necessary in such a disposition as his. The will is the thing that needs being brought in subjection.' And again: 'Now it seems to be an excellent discipline whereby daily some self-denial and command may be acquired in overcoming the repugnance to doing from duty that which has in itself no attraction.'

Mrs. Hare in this sentence did not express herself with her usual clarity. I think she must have meant that if Augustus, aged then five, was forced to do every day something he didn't want to do, he would eventually want to do it.

Once a year Maria took Augustus to stay with her parents at Stoke. They went in their own chariot, spending the night at post-inns, and even after the railway was built they continued to go in their chariot placed on a truck. When at last they came to use ordinary railway carriages they still had post-horses to meet them at a station near London, because Mrs. Hare would not have it known that she did anything so excessively improper as to enter London in a railway carriage.

Mrs. Leicester, Maria's step-mother, was severe but kind to Augustus. If he made a noise at home he was at once punished, but at Stoke Mrs. Leicester would say; 'Never mind the child, Maria, it is only innocent play.' She knew her duty as a clergyman's wife. She taught in the village school and when she thought it necessary to chastise her pupils, would take a book from the table and on using it say to the offender: 'You don't suppose I'm going to hurt my fingers in boxing your ears,' and then: 'Now we mustn't let the other ear be jealous,' upon which she soundly smacked it. The curates came to luncheon at the Rectory on Sundays, but they were not expected to talk, and if they ventured on a remark were snubbed. After they had eaten their cold veal they were called upon to give Mrs. Leicester an account of what they had been doing during the week, and if they had not done what she wished they were harshly chidden. They were obliged to come in by the back door, except Mr. Egerton, who was allowed to come in by the front door because he was a gentleman born. When Augustus told me this story, I, being young, was shocked.

'Don't be so silly,' he said when I expressed my indignation, 'it was perfectly natural. Mr. Egerton was a nephew of Lord Bridgewater. The others were nobodies. It would have been very impertinent of them to ring the front-door bell.'

'D'you mean to say that if they happened to come to the Rectory together, one would have gone to the front door and the other to the back?'

'Of course.'

'I don't think it speaks very well for Mr. Egerton.'

'I dare say you don't,' Augustus answered tartly. 'A gentleman knows his place and he takes it without giving it a second thought.'

Mrs. Leicester ruled the maids as strictly as she ruled the curates. When annoyed with them she had no hesitation in boxing their ears, which, such were the manners of the time, they never thought of resenting. The washing was done every three weeks and it was a rule of the house that it must begin at one in the morning. The ladies'-maids, who were expected to do the fine muslins, had to be at the wash-tubs at three. If one was late the housekeeper reported it to Mrs. Leicester, who gave her a good scolding. But Mrs. Leicester had a lighter side. Maria Hare thought it sinful to read fiction and in the evenings read Miss Strickland's *Queens of England* to her parents. *Pickwick* was coming out then in monthly numbers and Mrs. Leicester took them in. She read them in her dressing-room, behind closed doors, with her maid on the watch against intruders, and when she had finished a number she tore it up into little pieces which she threw in the waste-paper basket.

When Augustus was nine Mrs. Hare, on the insistence of the Misses Maurice, sent him to a preparatory school, and in the summer holidays, after the usual visit to Stoke, she took him for a tour of the English lakes. Uncle Julius accompanied them, and Maria, wishing to give Esther Maurice a rest after her arduous work at Reading, invited her to join the party. It was a dangerous kindness. Julius Hare proposed to Esther Maurice and was accepted. Maria Hare shed bitter tears when they told her of their engagement. Esther shed bitter tears and Julius 'sobbed and cried for days'. Ever since her husband's death Julius had been Maria's constant companion. He came to dinner at Lime every evening at six, leaving at eight, and Maria constantly drove up to the Rectory in the afternoon. Julius 'consulted her on every subject, and he thought every day a blank when they had no meeting.' Doubtless, since the Prayer Book and the laws of England forbade her to feel any warmer emotion for him, her affection remained strictly that of a sister-in-law for her brother-in-law, but she would have been more than human if she had welcomed the notion of another woman, a protégée of her own, becoming the mistress of Hurstmonceux Rectory. But however distasteful such a prospect was, she had a more serious objection to the marriage. Mr. Maurice was a scholar and a clergyman, but he was not a gentleman born, and the manners of the Misses Maurice, high-minded and worthy as they were, were not the sort of manners she was accustomed to. They were not ladies. Martin Stow perhaps was not a gentleman born, but her dear dead Augustus had been the first to admit his excellence and nobility of character. She loved him, but she had accepted her father's decision that he was not the sort of person it was proper for her to marry.

The marriage took place. Mrs. Julius Hare, now Aunt Esther to Augustus, was a deeply religious woman, but of a harsh and domineering character. 'She looked upon pleasure as a sin and if she felt that the affection for somebody drew her from the thorny path of self-sacrifice she tore that affection from her heart.' To such of the poor as accepted her absolute authority she was kind, generous and considerate; and to 'her husband, to whom her severe creed taught her to show the same inflexible obedience she exacted from others, she was utterly devoted.' For his soul's good she set herself to subdue the little Augustus. Since she was determined that her marriage should make no difference in the habits of the two families, and Julius had dined every night at Lime, she insisted that Maria Hare and Augustus should dine every night at the Rectory. In winter it was often impossible for them to go home after dinner and they passed the night at the Rectory. Augustus was a delicate boy and suffered badly from chilblains so that there were often large open sores on his hands and feet. Aunt Esther put him to bed in an unfurnished damp room with a deal trestle to sleep on, a straw palliasse and a single blanket. The servants were not allowed to bring him hot water and in the morning he had to break the ice in the pitcher with a brass candlestick or, if that had been taken away, with his wounded hands. Still for the good of his soul, because the smell of sauerkraut made him sick he was made to eat it. Sunday was a day of respite. Owing to her religious duties Maria Hare did not go to the Rectory, but Aunt Esther, fearing that Maria would indulge him, persuaded her to let Augustus be locked up in the vestry between services with a sandwich for his dinner. He had a cat to which he was devoted, and when Aunt Esther discovered this she insisted that it should be given up to her. Augustus wept, but Maria Hare said he must be taught to give up his own way and pleasures to others. With tears he took it to the Rectory and Aunt Esther had it hanged.

It is almost inconceivable that a pious, God-fearing woman could have treated a child of twelve with such inhumanity. I have wondered whether her behaviour to him, besides her determination to train him in the way of virtue and self-sacrifice, was not occasioned also by a desire, of which she may well have been unconscious, to give the adopted mother who adored him a needful lesson. Maria Hare had been very good to Esther Maurice, but had there not been something in her manner which never let the humble friend forget that Mrs. Hare was her benefactress and that there was a great gulf fixed between a young woman, of the highest principles certainly, but of humble origins, and Maria Leicester of Toft, the widow of a Hare of Hurstmonceux? Is it not possible that Esther Maurice, like Charlotte Brontë in her situation as a governess, saw slights when only kindness was intended, and in a dozen little ways felt that the subservience of her position was never entirely absent from Maria's mind? When she became Mrs. Julius Hare did it never cross her mind that it could only do dear Maria good to suffer? And she did suffer. But she accepted her distress at the miseries inflicted on the boy as a fiery trial that must be patiently endured.

I shall pass over the next few years of Augustus's life. On leaving his preparatory school, he went to Harrow, but owing to illness only stayed there for a year and until he was old enough to go to Oxford lived with tutors. He took his degree in 1857 and then started on the main business of his life. This was to paint in water-colours, see sights and mix in high society. He made his first sketch from nature when he was seven. Maria Hare drew well, and as she could not but look upon this accomplishment as harmless, she fostered Augustus's inclinations and gave him useful lessons. She would look at a drawing carefully and then say: 'And what does this line mean?'

'Oh, I thought it looked well.' 'Then, if you don't know exactly what it means, take it out at once.' This was sound advice. As Maria Hare deprecated colour, he was allowed to use only pencil and sepia, and it was not till he was grown up that she permitted him to paint in water-colour. He made endless sketches. The walls of Holmhurst were papered with the best of them in handsome frames and he had albums full of them. At this distance of time I cannot judge of their quality. Years later Maria Hare showed some of them to Ruskin, who examined them very carefully and at last pointed out one as the least bad of a very poor collection. Augustus had an eye for the picturesque and as I look back I have a suspicion that the critic was unduly severe. They were painted in the style of the mid-nineteenth century, and if they are still in existence might be found now to have a certain period charm.

III

When Augustus was only fourteen, at a tutor's at Lyncombe, he was already an indefatigable sight-seer. To visit an ancient house or a fine church he would often walk twenty-five miles a day. So that he should not be led astray Mrs. Hare sent him back to his tutor's with only five shillings in his pocket and he went on these excursions without a penny to buy himself a piece of bread. Many a time he sank down by the wayside, faint with hunger, and was glad to accept food from the 'common working people' he met on the road. But neither his delight in painting the picturesque nor his passion for sights was as important to him as to get into society. In this endeavour he started with certain advantages. Through his parents he was connected with a number of noble and county families, and through his adopted mother with several more. However distant the relationship he counted all their members as his cousins.

Maria Hare had been in poor health for some years and the doctors advised her to try living in a climate milder than that of Hurstmonceux. She had before this taken Augustus for short trips on the Continent, but soon after he left Oxford it was decided that they should make a prolonged sojourn abroad. So that they should be properly waited on they took Mrs. Hare's maid and manservant with them. Julius Hare, to the sorrow of his relations and the relief of his parishioners, had died two years before and Maria, while she was away, lent Lime to his widow. They travelled slowly, of course by carriage, through Switzerland and Italy, visiting places of interest and making abundant sketches; they had a goodly supply of books in their roomy chariot and during the journey read the 'whole of Arnold, Gibbon, Ranke and Milman'. It looks like a formidable undertaking. On reaching Rome they took an apartment in the Piazza del Popolo. Augustus's father had died some years before and his widow, whom Augustus called Italima, a contraction of Italian mamma, was living in Rome with her daughter Esmeralda. Of her two other sons, Francis and Robert, Augustus's elder brothers, one was in the Guards and the other in the Blues. Since he knew them but slightly and did not care for them I need only say that they lived as extravagantly as their father had done, with even smaller resources, and died destitute. Francis had further outraged his family by marrying 'a person with whom he had long been acquainted', which, I presume, was Augustus's delicate way of saying that she was his mistress. In his autobiography he dismissed her in a footnote: 'The person whom Francis Hare had married during the last months of his life vanished, immediately after his death, into the chaos from which she had come.'

Augustus had seen little of his real mother and she had never taken any interest in him. But now he became better acquainted with her. She moved with her daughter in the best Roman society, and when Maria Hare could spare him she took Augustus with her. The list of princes and princesses, dukes and duchesses, he thus frequented is impressive. Italima liked to see Augustus more often than his adopted mother quite approved of, and sometimes when he had a particular engagement with her, Maria Hare would demand his presence. It looks as though the saintly woman was not entirely devoid of the unpleasant failing of jealousy.

Maria Hare and Augustus remained abroad for eighteen months and would have remained longer but that Mrs. Hare began to suspect that her adopted son had leanings to Roman Catholicism, and though he was ill and the doctors told her he could not survive the rigour of an English winter she insisted on taking him back to a staunchly Protestant country. She felt that the hazard to his soul was of more consequence that the hazard to his body. She was well aware how much pleasure he took in the religious processions that so often passed through the streets of Rome, the sight of cardinals in their red robes driving in their coaches, the splendid ceremonies of the Church and the pomp of the Eternal City when the Pope was still a temporal sovereign. She knew Augustus well and she dreaded his levity. One day she told him that she had never known anyone who enjoyed things as much as he did; she said it not by way of blaming him, but perhaps with the feeling at the back of her mind that there was danger in such an attitude towards life.

During this period there was a wave of conversions to Catholicism. There had been the notorious instances of Newman and Manning; their example had been followed by others of lesser note, though by some of greater social importance, and it had caused dissension in many families. Italima and Esmeralda had become Catholics, though to Italima's credit it had to be admitted that she had sought to dissuade her daughter from taking the step, because she had expectations from her grandmother, Lady Anne Simpson, and the old lady would certainly disinherit her if she changed her religion. Sir John Paul, Augustus's grandfather, had turned his daughter out of the house and refused ever to see her again when she was received into the Church of Rome, and when Mary Stanley, Maria's niece and the daughter of the Bishop of Norwich, forsook the faith of her Protestant fathers, Maria could not but fear for her dear Augustus.

The reader will remember that from his earliest years he had been destined for the Church. It was on this account that Maria Hare had brought him up so strictly. It was on this account that he had been taught to sacrifice himself for others. It was on this account that his toys were taken away from him. It was on this account that Aunt Esther, when she came on the scene, had insisted that he should be inured to hardship and privation, and that he should learn that pleasure, a snare of the devil, was something he must eschew. Though the Hares had lost their land and most of their money, there still remained the rich living of Hurstmonceux, and as the youngest son of Francis Hare it was his right in due course to have it. Unfortunately Augustus's eldest brother had been driven by his financial necessities to sell the advowson, so that Maria Hare could never hope to see her adopted son occupy the Rectory with which she had so many pleasant and edifying associations, but that did not make it less desirable that Augustus should adopt the profession for which he had been so well prepared. His ancestry and his family connections marked him out to pursue the useful and profitable life of a clergyman who was a gentleman born. The founder of the family fortunes had held two bishoprics besides the Deanery of St. Paul's, one of Augustus's grandfathers had been Bishop of St. Asaph, another Canon of Winchester, his two uncles had taken Holy Orders; Maria's brother-in-law, Edward Stanley, had been Bishop of Norwich, and his son Arthur Stanley was already a Canon of Canterbury and would in due course no doubt occupy a position of even greater dignity. He did in fact become Dean of Westminster, marry Lady Augusta Bruce and grow to be a close friend of Queen Victoria. Then there were the Strathmores, the Ravensworths, the Stanleys of Alderley. With such connections Augustus could surely look forward to preferment. The good old days of pluralism were past, but there was no reason why with his ability and so many influential relations he should not achieve distinction in the Church.

It was a shock to Maria Hare when Augustus, while they were still in Italy, informed her, we can imagine how nervously, that he did not wish to be ordained. From every point of view, from the earthly as well as from the heavenly, this seemed as foolish as it was ungrateful. She shed bitter tears. But she was a sincerely Christian woman and what could she do when he told her that he felt himself unfitted to take Holy Orders? She loved him devotedly, and though it almost broke her heart, at last acquiesced in his determination. But when they got back to England and the family were informed, there was hell to pay. They asked him his reasons for refusing to be ordained. He could give none that was adequate. He merely said that it was uncongenial. Aunt Esther thought that made it all the more desirable that Maria should insist on it. Had he religious doubts? No. He had come back from Italy as true a Protestant as when he left. It was obvious then that if he persisted in his obstinacy it could only be that he wanted to lead an idle, useless life of self-indulgence.

The truth was simply that Augustus was bored with religion. He had been bored by the two services he had been forced to attend every Sunday and bored by the long, incomprehensible sermons of his Uncle Julius, bored by the elevating conversations on the power of faith which Maria Hare held with her friends and relations, exasperated by the evangelical fanaticism of the Maurice women and made miserable by the severities to which for his spiritual welfare he had been so long subjected. When I knew him Augustus had ceased going to church on Sundays, and if he continued to have family prayers it was as a social gesture becoming to a gentleman of ancient lineage.

Then came the question as to what he should do. He tried to get a clerkship at the Library of the British Museum, but did not succeed, and finally through the good offices of Arthur Stanley he was commissioned by John Murray to write the *Handbook of Berks, Bucks and Oxfordshire*. It was a job that just suited him, for it enabled him to do a great deal of sight-seeing and at the same time must bring him in contact with the sort of people he liked to know. He did in fact make a number of desirable acquaintances, discovered a number of new cousins and stayed at a number of grand houses. At about this time Lime was sold over Maria's head and she moved to Holmhurst, which then became Augustus's home for the rest of his life. The handbook was so well received that Murray asked him to choose any counties he liked for another work of the same kind. He chose Northumberland and Durham. So began the long series of guide-books which made the name of Augustus Hare well-known to at least two generations of travellers in Europe. They were written on a plan that had novelty, for interspersed with useful information were long quotations from the New Testament, Fathers of the Church, historians, art critics and poets. The earnest sightseer must have been flattered to find in his guide-book quotations from Virgil, Horace, Ovid, Martial, Suetonius, and even from a work which few can have read, Prudentius *contra Symmachum*. Augustus paid his readers the compliment of leaving these passages untranslated and the compliment was doubtless appreciated.

But his habit of extensively quoting from other authors sometimes got him into trouble. In his *Cities of Northern and Central Italy* he quoted largely from some articles by Freeman, the historian, without receiving permission, whereupon Freeman charged him with bare-faced and wholesale robbery. Augustus was very much hurt. He felt that the real interest of Freeman's articles had been overlooked owing to the 'dogmatic and verbose style in which they were written', and he had introduced extracts from them in order to attract notice to them and so do the historian a good turn. 'I need hardly say,' he adds in a footnote to his account of the incident, 'that as soon as possible thereafter I eliminated all reference to Mr. Freeman, and all quotations from his works from my books.' He was satisfied that he had thus swept the historian back into the obscurity from which he had delivered him. What Augustus describes as a most virulent and abusive article appeared upon this work in the *Athenœum*, in which he was accused of having copied from Murray's *Handbooks* without acknowledgement and as proof quoting passages in which the same curious mistake occurred. And in fact that is exactly what he had done. But the books were very popular. By the end of the nineteenth century there had been fifteen editions of *Walks in Rome*, five of *Florence and Venice*, and six of *Walks in London* and *Wanderings in Spain*. Spain, Holland and Scandinavia, all of which he wrote books about, he knew very superficially, but he knew Italy and France as few people did then or are likely to do now.

During the next ten years Maria and Augustus Hare spent a great deal of time in France and Italy. She was often ill and, when she was, Augustus nursed her devotedly. In the intervals he moved in high circles, took parties of well-born ladies to paint in watercolour with him, and in Rome conducted them on sight-seeing tours during which, the centre of a little crowd of admiring females, he discoursed on the artistic merit and the historical associations of the objects he showed them.

Italima had been greatly reduced in circumstances by

the failure of her father's bank and lost what she had left by
the defalcation of the attorney who attended to her affairs.
She died in 1864. Her daughter Esmeralda died four years
later and Maria Hare in 1870. For a while after this event
Augustus was in acute financial anxiety, for the relation
between his adopted mother and himself had been so close
that she could not bring herself to believe that he would
long survive her. She failed in consequence to make what
he calls the usual arrangements for his future provision,
and it looked as though he would be left with nothing but
Holmhurst and sixty pounds a year. He does not explain
how things were arranged, but the upshot seems to have
been that he succeeded to her fortune. He complained
bitterly that, since he was no legal relation, he had to
pay ten per cent duty on everything he inherited. He
was always reticent about his income and I have no
notion what it was; it was sufficient to enable him to
keep up Holmhurst in some style, entertain constantly,
and travel whenever he had a mind to. He had at least
enough to lose a few hundred pounds now and then on
a wild-cat speculation. He did not look upon himself
as a professional author, but as a gentleman who from
purely altruistic motives wrote books which would help
travellers profitably to enjoy the beauties of nature and
art. He published them at his own expense and they must
have brought him in considerable sums.

From the time of Maria Hare's death Augustus's life
followed a course of some regularity. He went abroad a
good deal, generally for his work on the guide-books;
and when in England he spent some time at Holmhurst,
receiving a succession of guests, and made a round of
country house visits. When in London he had a bedroom
in Jermyn Street and went to the Athenaeum for breakfast,
where he always occupied the same table; he spent the
morning at work in the library and went out to lunch;
in the afternoon there were calls to pay, a tea-party or
a reception at which he had to make *acte de présence*,

and at night he dined out. There is a note in his Journal which strikes a sinister note: 'May 15. Drawing-party in dirty, picturesque St. Bartholomew's. For the first time this year no one asked me to dinner, and I was most profoundly bored.' Augustus never married. There is a cryptic remark in his autobiography which suggests that on one occasion he had an inclination to do so. 'This year (1864) I greatly wished something that was not compatible with the entire devotion of my time and life to my mother. Therefore I smothered the wish, and the hope that had grown up with it.' If this means what I think it does I should say it was safe to surmise that the object of his affections was a well-connected young woman of some fortune; but of course he was financially dependent on Maria Hare, and though there is no reason to believe that his reasons for smothering the wish were not such as he said, he cannot but have been aware that if he married without her consent she was capable of cutting him off without a shilling. It was a tradition in the family. I do not think he was of a passionate nature. He told me once that he had never had sexual intercourse till he was thirty-five. He marked the occasions on which this happened, about once every three months, with a black cross in his Journal. But this is a matter on which most men are apt to boast, and I dare say that to impress me he exaggerated the frequency of his incontinence.

During the last months of Mrs. Hare's life Augustus had discussed with her his desire to write a book about her which should be called *Memorials of a Quiet Life*. She laughed at the notion when first he put it before her, but after reflecting for a day or two said that she could not oppose his wish if he thought that the simple experiences of her life, and God's guidance in her case, might be made useful to others; she gave him many journals and letters which he might use, and directed the arrangement of others. He set to work at once and was able to read to her the earlier chapters before she died. He spent the winter after her death in seclusion until he had finished the book. His cousins, especially the Stanleys, were very angry when they found out what he was up to, and even threatened to bring an action against him if he published any of the letters of Mrs. Stanley, Maria's sister. Arthur Stanley, by this time Dean of Westminster, went so far as to persuade John Murray to go to Augustus's publishers to try to stop the publication. The book was issued and three days after its appearance a second edition was called for. It was in fact a great success both in England and in the United States, and pilgrims came from America to visit the various places Augustus had written about. Carlyle, whom he met at luncheon, told him: 'I do not often cry and am not much given to weeping, but your book is most profoundly touching, and when the dear Augustus (Maria's husband) was making the hay I felt a lesson deep down in my heart.'

The world that read these two stout volumes with emotion has long ceased to exist. To me they have seemed tedious. There is, of course, a great deal about the Hares and the Leicesters; the members of the two families wrote immensely long letters to one another, and one can only marvel at the patience they must have had to read them. The pious consolations, the pious exhortations which these people wrote to one another on the death of a relation or a friend were so unctuous that one can hardly believe in their sincerity. But one must not judge of the sentiments of one generation by those of another. God was constantly in their thoughts and their conversation turned frequently on the life to come, but Augustus somewhat maliciously noticed that though in youth they talked of longing, pining for 'the coming of the Kingdom', as they grew older they seemed less eager for it. 'By and by would do.'

The success of *Memorials of a Quiet Life* brought Augustus other work of the same kind, and in course of time he published *Life and Letters of Frances, Baroness*

Bunsen, *The Story of Two Noble Lives, The Gurneys of Earlham*, and others. The subjects of *The Story of Two Noble Lives* were Louisa, Lady Waterford and Charlotte, Lady Canning. It is still readable; indeed the chapters that deal with the period during which their father, Lord Stuart de Rothesay, was ambassador in Paris, from 1815 to 1830, are very interesting. Augustus had made the acquaintance of Lady Waterford when he was getting together his material for Murray's *Handbook on Durham and Northumberland;* and after this he paid her a yearly visit first at Ford and then at High-cliffe. This was not an isolated case. He was apparently a welcome guest at a vast number of great houses, and there seem to have been few to which he could not count on an invitation year after year. He went from castle to castle, from park to park and from hall to hall. He was not what people call a man's man. He could play no games. He had never touched a card in his life. He neither shot, fished nor hunted. Though he had a few male friends of his own age, men he had known at Oxford, and a few others whose religious proclivities he could sympathise with, the men with whom he got on best were older. They liked the enthusiastic interest he took in their noble mansions and their contents. Sometimes, however, his enthusiasm was put to a more severe test than he appreciated. When he went to stay at Port Eliot his host met him at the station and almost walked him off his feet while he showed him every picture in the house, every plant in the garden and every walk in the woods. 'There is a limit to what ought to be shown,' Augustus wrote acidly in his diary, 'and Lord Eliot has never found it out.'

It was with the ladies that Augustus found himself most at ease. They liked to go sketching with him, they were flattered by his eagerness to see the local sights and took him daily for drives to visit a neighbouring great house, a fine church or a romantic ruin. In those days, days long before the gramophone and the radio, when the gentlemen came home from their day's sport, after tea the ladies retired to rest till it was time to dress for dinner and Augustus went to his room to write his Journal. The interval between dinner and bedtime was devoted to conversation and music. Augustus showed the party his sketches and those who sketched showed him theirs. Anyone who played the piano was invited to play and anyone who had a voice was pressed to sing. It was then that Augustus came into his own. He was a famous teller of stories. He had discovered his gift when he was a boy at Harrow and early in life had begun assiduously to collect them. He wrote them all down in his Journal. A great many were ghost stories, for there were few of the houses he visited that did not harbour a ghost who appeared either to frighten a guest who had been put in the haunted room or to announce the death of a member of the family. There appears to be a lack of initiative in the conduct of ghosts and there is a certain tediousness in their behaviour; Augustus, however, told his stories very well and when people asked him whether he believed in them he answered that he had no doubt at all of their existence. A little shudder of apprehension would pass through his listeners. But ghost stories by no means exhausted his repertoire. He could tell stories of telepathy, of clairvoyance and of precognition. He could tell blood-curdling tales about the Italian and Spanish aristocracy. It was a 'turn' that he did, and he took pains to perfect himself. In fact it was the greatest of his social assets. He relates that when he was staying at Raby, if ever he escaped to his room after tea a servant would tap on the door and say: 'Their Graces want you to come down again.' 'Always,' he adds, 'from their insatiable love of stories.' His renown grew to such a height that on one occasion a party was arranged at Holland House so that he might tell Princess Louise some of his stories, 'which she had graciously wished to hear'.

The houses he visited were mostly those of highminded

people and the conversation often turned on religious subjects. On these Augustus, who had heard them discussed at home from his earliest youth, was quite at home. Sometimes, however, his hosts went to lengths that he thought unnecessary. When, for instance, he was staying with the George Liddells he found Sunday 'a severe day'. It was spent in going to church, reading prayers and listening to long sermons at home. Even on week-days, after morning prayers, the Psalms and Lessons for the day, verse by verse, were read before anyone was allowed to go out.

Augustus did not consort much with men of letters and I think his interest in them was only in so far as they gave occasion for an anecdote which he could tell at the luncheon or the dinner table. On one of her journeys Maria Hare took him to see Wordsworth, who read to him, 'admirably', some of his verses. Augustus said that the poet talked a good deal about himself and his own poems, 'and I have a sense of his being not vain, but conceited.' The distinction is delicate and I think Augustus must have meant that Wordsworth had an overweening opinion of himself without caring much what other people thought of him. We are all more tolerant of vanity than of conceit, for the vain man is sensitive to our opinion of him and thereby flatters our self-esteem; the conceited man is not and thereby wounds it.

Mrs. Greville took Augustus to see Tennyson: 'Tennyson is older looking than I expected so that his *unkempt* appearance signifies less. He has an abrupt, bearish manner, and seems thoroughly hard and *un*poetical: one would think of him as a man in whom the direct prose of life was absolutely ingrained.' Tennyson insisted that Augustus should tell him some stories, but he 'was atrociously bad audience and constantly interrupted with questions.' 'On the whole,' Augustus adds, 'the wayward poet leaves a favourable impression. He could scarcely be less egotistic with all the flattery he has . . .' 'Mr. Browning', whom he met at Lady Castletoun's, failed to make an impression on him, though he quotes, I suspect with approval, Lockhart's remark: 'I like Robert so much because he is not a damned literary person.' Carlyle had been to stay at Hurstmonceux Rectory, where 'they had not liked him very much', when Augustus was a child, and during the period with which I am now concerned he met him from time to time in London. Once Lady Ashburton took him to see the sage of Chelsea in Cheyne Row. 'He complained much of his health, fretting and fidgeting about himself, and said that he could form no worse wish for the devil than that he might be able to give him his stomach to digest with through all eternity.' On another occasion, at Lady Ashburton's, Carlyle 'talked in volumes, with fathomless depths of adjectives, into which it was quite impossible to follow him, and in which he himself often got out of his depth.' Augustus met Oscar Wilde at Madame du Quaine's. 'He talked in a way intended to be very startling, but she startled him by saying quietly, "You poor dear foolish boy, how can you talk such nonsense?" Another friend had met him at a country house and one day he came down looking very pale. "I am afraid you are ill, Mr. Wilde," said one of the party. "No, not ill, only tired," he answered. "The fact is, I picked a primrose in the wood yesterday, and it was so ill, I have been sitting up with it all night."'

So much for Augustus's association with men of letters. When he was still quite a young man he had been impressed by the Speaker of the House of Commons, Denison, with whom he was a fellow-guest at Winton Castle, because he had 'a wonderful fund of agreeable small talk.' Augustus realised how useful an accomplishment this was. I don't know whether he deliberately sought to acquire it, but from my own recollection I can vouch for his having done so. If he could dine out every night he was in London it was because he gave his hosts good value for their money. He could listen as well as talk. I think one can get some idea of the sort of conversation which was then in favour by an incident Augustus relates. Rogers, the banker-poet, was a great talker and there was a brash young man by the name of Monckton Milnes, whom people called The Cool of the Evening, and who was a great talker too. 'If Milnes began to talk, Rogers would look at him sourly, and say, "Oh, you want to hold forth, do you?" and then, turning to the rest of the party, "I am looking for my hat, Mr. Milnes is going to entertain the company."' But by the time Augustus came to know the brash young man he had become Lord Houghton, and 'in spite of his excessive vanity' he grew sincerely attached to him. He could not but deplore that Lord Houghton sometimes entertained 'a quaint collection of anybodies and nobodies'; on one occasion indeed he asked Augustus to a party where he met 'scarcely anyone but authors, and a very odd collection – Black, Yates, and James the novelists; Sir Francis Doyle and Swinburne the poets; Mrs. Singleton, the exotic poetess (Violet Fane), brilliant with diamonds; Mallock, who had suddenly become a lion from having written a clever squib called "The New Republic", and Mrs. Julia Ward Howe with her daughter'. This was not the sort of company Augustus was used to keep.

Lord Houghton could tell as many stories as he could and had a fund of small talk as agreeable. Augustus was wise enough not to compete with him. But it was different when he came in contact with persons of no social consequence who sought to make themselves heard at the dinner tables of the great. Abraham Hayward, whom he often to his disapproval met in society, he dismisses in two footnotes: 'Constantly invited by a world which feared him, he was always determined to be listened to, and generally said something worth hearing'; but nothing that Augustus thought fit to record. In another footnote Augustus says that Hayward, 'who had been articled in early life to an obscure country attorney, always seemed to consider it the *summum bonum* of life to dwell among the aristocracy as a man of letters; and in this he succeeded admirably, and was always witty and well-informed, usually satirical, and often very coarse.'

IV

Augustus's social career was crowned by an event that came about through his writing of the memoirs of the Baroness Bunsen. When this work was approaching completion he went to Germany to see her two unmarried daughters and on the way paid a long visit to the Dowager Princess of Wied, who had been a close friend of hers. Here he met her sister, the Queen of Sweden, who told him that she must consider him a friend, since in a life of trouble his *Memorials of a Quiet Life* had been a great comfort to her and that she never went anywhere without them. She was sending the Prince Royal to Rome that winter 'to learn his world' and expressed a wish that Augustus should go there too. She invited him to visit her in Sweden and shortly afterwards he did so. He made a good impression on the King and it was agreed that Augustus should act as guide and mentor to the Prince during his sojourn in the Eternal City. The Queen begged him to sow some little seeds of good in her son's young heart and the King talked to him of the places and people he should see. Augustus accordingly went to Rome for the winter. He saw the Prince twice a day and showed him the necessary sights. He took care that he should make acquaintance with the right people. He read English with him and delivered lectures at places of interest not only attended by the Prince and Baron Holtermann, Marshal of the Palace, but by a choice selection of distinguished persons. At the end of the winter Augustus was able to write: 'On looking back, I have unmixed satisfaction that I came. He leaves Rome quite a different person from the

Prince I found here – much strengthened, and I am sure much improved in character as well as speaking English and French (which he did not know before), and being able to take a lively animated part in a society in which he was previously a cypher.'

In May the Prince arrived with his suite at Claridge's. Augustus took him to see the Royal Academy, the National Gallery, the Tower of London and accompanied him to Oxford, where he was given an honorary degree. Throughout the season he went to a great many parties, where royalties, English and German, were present in numbers, dukes and duchesses past counting, and in fact everyone who was anyone. At a ball at Lady Salisbury's Augustus presented so many of his relations to the Prince that he said what astonished him more than anything in England was the multitude of Mr. Hare's cousins.

The years wore on. Augustus continued to travel, to go to house parties, and when in London to dine out. The period when visits to country houses often lasted weeks, and even months, was long since a thing of the past. It was become usual to have guests for the weekend. Augustus rarely accepted such invitations; he preferred to spend his Sundays in London. He went to church to hear the preacher who was the fashion of the day, and then, perhaps after a stroll in the Park, went out to lunch. Luncheon parties on Sunday, not yet quite killed by the week-end habit of going into the country, were popular. The most famous of these were given by Lady Dorothy Neville and to them Augustus often went. In the afternoon there was generally a tea-party to go to, and someone was sure to ask him to dinner or supper.

But even dukes and duchesses are mortal. The day comes when the chatelaines of great castles are displaced by their daughters-in-law and either retire to a dower house or establish themselves in Bath or Bournemouth. Augustus began to spend more time at Holmhurst, and was apt to come up to London only when a brilliant marriage or an important funeral made it necessary. The company he kept was not so choice as it had been. He had never much frequented that of Americans or Jews. In his early years he found the Americans he met on his travels vulgar, but he grew more tolerant with age, and when Mr. Astor bought Cliveden and asked him to stay he thought him genial and unassuming. Money was becoming a power. Aforetime, when a person of title married the daughter of a wealthy manufacturer, Augustus, on mentioning the fact, passed it over lightly and it was almost with surprise that he noted in his Journal that the new countess was unaffected and ladylike. Now not only younger sons but heirs to great titles were marrying into Jewish families.

The nineties came. Augustus did not like them. He was getting on for sixty and many of his old friends had died. The pace of life had increased. A different generation amused itself in a different way. There were no longer ladies of artistic inclinations to go on a drawing-party with him to 'dirty, picturesque St. Bartholomew's'; there were no longer ladies of high rank with whom he could have edifying conversation on religious subjects; no longer could he spend pleasant evenings with his portfolio showing his sketches to an appreciative circle, and no longer was he pressed to tell his famous stories. There was no more conversation. The size and lateness of dinners had killed society. The time had passed when a brilliant talker could 'hold forth' and the company was prepared to listen. Now everybody wanted to talk and nobody wanted to listen. Perhaps Augustus was beginning to seem a bit of a bore; and as the decade wore on there was more than one evening in the year when no one asked him to dinner. He had an affectionate disposition, and by the time I came to know him he still had a number of friends who were attached to him, but when they spoke of him it was with as it were a shrug of the shoulders, with a smile kindly enough, but with a suspicion of apology. He had become faintly ridiculous.

35

The reader can hardly have read so far without its having crossed his mind that Augustus was something of a snob. He was. But before I deal with this I should like to point out that the word has in the course of years somewhat changed its significance. When Augustus was young, gentlemen 'wore straps to their trousers, not only when riding, but always: it was considered the *ne plus ultra* of snobbism to appear without them' (so in the days of my own youth it was considered to wear brown boots in London). I take it that when Augustus wrote this, snobbish was equivalent to vulgar or common. I have a notion that the sense it now has was given it by Thackeray. Of course Augustus was a snob. But here, like Thomas Diafoirus in *Le Malade Imaginaire*, I am inclined to say: *'Distinguo, Mademoiselle.'* The Oxford Dictionary defines the snob as 'one who meanly or vulgarly admires and seeks to imitate, or associate with, those of superior rank or wealth; one who wishes to be regarded as a person of social importance.' Well, Augustus didn't *wish* to be regarded as a person of social importance; it had never occurred to him that he was anything else. Not to have regarded him as such would have seemed to him merely a proof of your crass ignorance. He did not meanly or vulgarly seek to associate with those of superior rank. His grandfather was Mr. Hare-Naylor of Hurstmonceux, and he counted at least three Earls as his cousins, several times removed certainly, but cousins none the less. He had always moved in the highest circles of society, indeed it was for them that he had written one of his most successful books, *The Story of Two Noble Lives*, and he regarded no one as his superior. He had not, like Abraham Hayward, wormed his way into those circles by intelligence, or wit, but taken his place in them by right of birth. Yet most people looked upon Augustus as an outrageous snob.

On one occasion, after I had known him for some years, I happened to be at a party when the conversation turned upon this trait of his, not with malice, but with an amused indulgence. At that time when you had dined out it was polite to call within a week, and though you hoped to find your hostess not at home it was only decent to ask whether she was. Sometimes, in my nervousness, when the butler opened the door to me I could not for the life of me remember the name of the lady on whom I was paying this visit of courtesy. I spoke of this and added that when I told Augustus how great my embarrassment was when this occurred, he answered: 'Oh, but that often happens to me, but I just say, "Is her ladyship at home?" and it's always right.' Everyone laughed and said: 'How exactly like Augustus!' I was somewhat taken aback when twenty years later I read this little quip of mine in a book of memoirs, for there was not a word of truth in it; I had invented it on the spur of the moment merely to amuse the company. But it was sufficiently characteristic of Augustus to be remembered. I have written this essay partly to make reparation to his memory.

It was inexcusable of me thus to make fun of Augustus, because his kindness to me was great. He took an interest in my career as a novelist. 'The only people worth writing about,' he told me, 'are the lower classes and the upper. No one wants to read about the middle classes.' He could not have foreseen that a time would come when, so low has the stock of the upper classes fallen, no self-respecting novelist would introduce a person of rank into his fiction except as a figure of fun. Augustus felt that as a medical student at St. Thomas's Hospital I must have learnt as much as was needful about the lower orders, but he thought I should acquire more than a superficial knowledge of the manners and customs of the nobility and gentry. With this object in view he took me to call on various of his old friends, and finding I had not made too bad an impression, asked them to invite me to their parties. I was glad enough to have the opportunity to enter a world new to me. It was not the great world, for by then Augustus had lost touch with it; it was a world of elderly gentle-folk who lived in discreet, rather dull splendour. I was no credit to Augustus and if they continued to invite me it was for his sake rather than for mine. Like most young men, then and now, I thought my youth a sufficient contribution to the entertainment of the company. I had not learnt that when you go to a party it is your business to do your best to add to its success. I was silent and even if I had had anything to say would have been too shy to say it. But I kept my eyes and my ears open, and I learnt one or two things that I have since found worth knowing. I was once at a great dinner of twenty-four people in Portland Place. Of course all the men were in tails and white ties and the women, in satins and velvets, with long trains, were richly jewelled. We walked down the stairs to the dining-room in a long procession, giving our arm to the lady whom we had been instructed to 'take down'. The table blazed with old silver, cut glass and flowers out of season. The dinner was long and elaborate. At the end of it the ladies, on catching the hostess's eye, rose and trooped up to the drawing-room, leaving the men to drink coffee and liqueurs, smoke and discuss the affairs of the nation. I found myself sitting then next to an old gentleman whom I knew to be the Duke of Abercorn. He asked me my name and, when I gave it, said: 'I'm told you're a very clever young man.' I made an appropriately modest reply, and he took out of his tail pocket a large cigar-case.

'Do you like cigars?' he asked me, as he opened it and displayed to my view a number of handsome Havanas.

'Very much,' I said.

I didn't see fit to tell him that I couldn't afford to buy them and smoked one only when it was offered me.

'So do I,' he said, 'and when I come to dinner with a widow lady I always bring my own. I advise you to do the same.'

He looked carefully over those in his case, picked one

out, put it up to his ear and slightly pressed it to see that it was in perfect condition, and then snapped the case shut and put it back in his pocket. It was good advice he gave me, and since I have been in a position to do so I have taken it.

Augustus, though indulgent, did not spare reproof when he thought it was good for me. One Tuesday morning, when I had been spending the week-end with him, the post brought me a letter which he must have written soon after my departure. 'My dear Willie,' it ran. 'Yesterday when we came in from our walk you said you were thirsty and asked for a *drink*. I have never heard you vulgar before. A gentleman does *not* ask for a *drink*, he asks for *something to drink*. Yours affectionately. Augustus.'

Dear Augustus! I'm afraid that if he were alive now he would find the whole English-speaking world as vulgar as he found me then.

On another occasion when I told him I had been somewhere by bus, he said stiffly: 'I prefer to call the conveyance to which you refer an omnibus'; and when I protested that if he wanted a cab he didn't ask for a cabriolet, 'Only because people are so uneducated today they wouldn't understand,' he retorted. Augustus was of opinion that manners had sadly deteriorated since his youth. Few young men knew how to behave in polite society, and how could you wonder when there was no longer anyone to teach them? In this connection he was fond of telling a story about Caroline, Duchess of Cleveland. She had rented Osterley and had a number of people staying with her. She was lame and walked with an ebony stick. One day when they were all sitting in the drawing-room the duchess got up, and a young man, thinking she wanted to ring the bell, sprang to his feet and rang it for her; where-upon she hit him angrily over the head with her stick and said: 'Sir, officiousness is not politeness.' 'And quite right too,' said

Augustus, and then in an awe-struck tone: 'For all he knew she might have wanted to go to the water-closet.' Even duchesses are subject, his lowered voice indicated, to natural necessities. 'She was a very great lady,' he added. 'She's the last woman who ever smacked her footman's face in Bond Street.' He thought with nostalgia of his own grand-mother, the wife of the Reverend Oswald Leicester, who habitually boxed the ears of her maids. Those were the brave days of old, when servants were prepared to suffer corporal punishment at the hands of their mistresses.

Augustus published the first three volumes of *The Story of My Life* in 1896 and the next three in 1900. Seldom can a work have been received with such a unanimity of hostile criticism, and it is true that one might cavil at an autobiography even of a very great man in six volumes of nearly five hundred pages each. The *Saturday Review* described it as a monument of self-sufficiency and found it wholly without delicacy. The *Pall Mall Gazette* was filled with genuine pity for a man who could attach importance to a life so trivial. The *National Observer* had not for long met with an author so garrulous and so self-complacent. *Blackwood* asked: 'What is Mr. Augustus Hare?' Mr. Augustus Hare remained superbly indifferent. He had written the book for himself and his relations, as he had written *The Story of Two Noble Lives* for 'the upper circles of society', and not for the general public, and I suppose it never occurred to him that in that case it might have been better to print it privately. Even after the publication of the second three volumes, undeterred he went on with the story, writing every morning, to the very end of his life. There was no one, however, with sufficient piety to publish what was doubtless a bulky manuscript.

To refresh my memory I have recently re-read *The Story of My Life*. What the reviewers said was true enough, but it was not the whole truth. It was apparently the custom of the day when you went abroad to write long descriptions to your friends of the sights you saw, and these letters of his Augustus printed in full. They are tedious. Yet they describe a way of travel, by carriage or *vetturino*, which no longer obtains, and the look of old towns and historic cities the aspect and character of which the advance of civilisation has entirely changed. If a novelist wanted to write a story situated in Rome during the last years of the temporal power he would find in Augustus's pages not a little picturesque material that he could turn to good use. Of course the lists of important persons he met on his visits to great houses are intolerably dull. He had no gift for bringing people to life and they exist merely as names; though not himself a sayer of good things, he had a quick appreciation of those said by others, and a diligent reader is often rewarded by coming upon a nice repartee. I should have liked to be present when the lady on being reproached for burning the candle at both ends, said: 'Why, I thought that was the very way to make both ends meet.' Augustus inserted in the six volumes of this work all the stories, ghost stories and others, which he used to relate to a group of spellbound ladies of high rank. Some of them are very good. It is unfortunate that they should be buried in a mass of twaddle. Augustus suffered from the persuasion that he was a gentleman, and an author, though a voluminous one, only by the way. If he had been a man of letters first and a gentleman next, he might, instead of writing the six volumes of his autobiography, with the material at his disposal have produced two or three books which would have been, not a lively, but at least an interesting, picture of the times.

V

Augustus had suffered from an affection of the heart for some years, and one morning, in 1903, when the maid went into his room to bring him his cup of tea and his two slices of thin bread and butter, she found him lying on the floor in his night-shirt, dead.

Zurbaran

I

Long ago, in the dim past of the thirteenth century, when Alfonso the Wise was King of Castile, some herdsmen were guarding their cattle near a place called Halia in Estremadura. One of them missed a cow that belonged to him and went to look for her, but after vainly ranging the plain for three days, he thought it well to pursue his search in the mountains, and there, not far from the River Guadalupe, he found her lying dead in a great grove of oak trees. He was surprised that the wolves had not mangled the carcase, and bewildered when he found no wound or injury to account for the creature's death. To make the best of a bad job, he took out his knife to skin it and, as the custom was, began by making two cuts on the chest in the form of a cross; upon which the cow rose to her feet, and the herdsman, terror-stricken, started away from her. As he did so Our Lady St. Mary the Virgin appeared to him and spoke as follows:

'Have no fear, for I am the Mother of God, through whom the race of mankind was redeemed. Take your cow and put her with the others, for from her you will get many more in memory of the apparition which you now see. And when you have put her with the others, go back to your dwelling-place and tell the priests and the people there to come to this place where I have appeared to you, and let them dig and they will find an image of me.'

The Blessed Virgin vanished from his sight, and the herdsman took his cow and put her with the others and

43

told his companions what had happened to him. They jeered, but he answered and said:

'My friends, do not believe what I say, but believe the sign on the chest of the cow.'

Then they, seeing the sign in the form of a cross, believed him. He left them to return to his village, and as he went told whomsoever he met of the strange thing that had occurred to him. The cowherd was a native of Caceres, where he had a wife and children, and when he came to his house he found his wife weeping because her son was dead, whereupon he said:

'Do not be troubled nor weep, for I promise him to St. Mary of Guadalupe if she will restore him to me alive and well, and I will give him to be the servant of her house.'

And at that moment the boy rose, alive and well, and said to his father:

'Father, get ready, and let us go to St. Mary of Guadalupe.'

They that were there were amazed and believed all that the cowherd told them of the apparition of Our Lady. Then he went to the priests and said to them:

'Gentlemen, know that St. Mary the Virgin appeared to me in the mountains near the River Guadalupe; and she bade me tell you to go to that place and dig there, and you would find an image of her, and that you should take it from there and build her a house. And she told me further that those who were in charge of her house should give food once a day to all of the poor who came to it. And she told me further that she would make many people come to her house from many countries on account of the many miracles she would perform all over the world both on sea and on land. And she told me further that there, on that great mountain, she would cause a town to be built.'

No sooner had the priests, and others, heard these things than they betook themselves to the place where Our Lady had appeared. And when they got there they dug and found a cave like a sepulchre and they took the image of Our Lady which was there, and they built a little house of dry stones and of green wood for her, and they roofed it with cork because in that district there were many cork trees. Then the sick, suffering from various ills, came to that spot, and when they prayed to the image of Our Lady they were healed; and they returned to their own countries praising God and his blessed Mother for the great marvels and miracles she had performed. And the cowherd remained with his wife and children as guardian of the shrine, and his descendants as servitors of St. Mary the Virgin.

The attentive reader will have noticed that the cowherd, when he came to tell his story to the priests, somewhat enlarged upon the instructions which the Blessed Virgin had given him, and thus secured for himself a position of honour and perhaps of profit. The inhabitants of Estremadura have the reputation in Spain of being as canny as they are adventurous.

Notwithstanding that the sanctuary was in a wild and almost inaccessible place pilgrims came from afar off to do reverence to the image on account of the miracles and marvels which by means of it St. Mary performed. In course of time the little sanctuary fell into decay, and Alfonso XI, grandson of Alfonso the Wise, built in its place a great church so that all who came might find room to worship. At about this time he fought a desperate battle with the Moors, and in danger of defeat placed his cause in the hands of St. Mary of Guadalupe, who thereupon granted him a glorious victory. From then on, the Kings of Castile, and afterwards the Kings of Spain, showed great devotion to the sanctuary. They endowed it with lands, as also did private persons, and gradually it acquired great wealth. Houses were built for the priests, hospitals for the sick, dormitories for the pilgrims; and since their needs had to be provided for, Jews and Moors, in whose hands trade then was, lured by the prospect of gain, settled in the town which was built to accommodate them. Guadalupe underwent various vicissitudes, for its vast estates, its immense herds, the privileges which had been accorded it, excited the jealousy of neighbouring feudal lords, lay and ecclesiastic, and more than once it had to resist the assault of armed bands. Notwithstanding, by means of pious donations and the ability of its priors, its wealth increased. Towards the end of the fourteenth century the monks of the order of St. Jerome were charged with its custody and administration. Succeeding priors erected buildings of great splendour and spent enormous sums on their decoration. Kings continued to visit and befriend it. Christopher Columbus before his first journey went there to ask for the protection of the Blessed Virgin; later, Cortez, Pizarro and Balboa, all natives of Estremadura, went to thank Our Lady for the favours she had conferred upon them.

Now, early in the thirties of the seventeenth century, Philip IV being then King of Spain, Fray Diego de Montalvo, the prior, decided to build a sacristy more magnificent than any in Spain, and he engaged a painter called Francisco de Zurbaran to paint pictures to adorn its walls. He chose him doubtless because he had already won reputation for his paintings of monks, especially those who wore a white habit, as did those of St. Jerome, and perhaps also because he was a native of Estremadura. He was born in fact in a tiny village called Fuente de Cantos not very far from Guadalupe.

The date of Zurbaran's birth is unknown, but his certificate of baptism still exists, and this is dated November the seventh, 1598. His father was a peasant in easy circumstances and, like the peasant in Fuente de Cantos to this day, had, it may be supposed, a two-storey house in the village street, with unglazed windows, and he kept his cow and his pigs, his goats and his donkey on the ground floor, and lived in the upper one. While he attended to his land, the boy of a morning led the livestock to the pasture, and it is related that one day, when he was but twelve, some gentlemen who were hunting saw him drawing on the trunks of trees with a piece of charcoal, and struck by his cleverness took him to Seville. But stories more or less similar have been told of various painters, of Giotto among others, and are merely an expression of the surprise laymen must feel when they discover talent in someone whose birth and antecedents give no reason for it. Talent is a mysterious gift of nature for which there is no accounting.

The story told of Zurbaran cannot be true, since there is a document extant which proves that he did not go to Seville till he was between fifteen and sixteen. This is an agreement, signed by his father towards the end of 1613, whereby he apprenticed his son for three years to a certain Pedro Diaz de Villanueva, who is described as an *imaginero*, a maker of images, and who by affixing his signature to the document early in January undertook to teach Francisco de Zurbaran his art such as he knew it without concealing anything from him, for which he was to receive sixteen ducats, half payable at once and the other half at the end of eighteen months. The ducat was worth about ten shillings, but ten shillings then was equivalent to five pounds or more today, so that the total sum paid would amount now to something between eighty and a hundred pounds. The agreement stipulated that for this the image-maker should provide his apprentice with board and lodging and pay for his treatment in sickness so long as this did not last longer than two weeks, in which case the expense was to be borne by the boy's father. His father was besides to provide him with clothes and foot-wear. A further condition was that if 'the said Francisco' during the three years of his apprenticeship chose to work on feast-days and holidays his earnings should belong to him.

Some surprise has been occasioned by the fact that the lad should have been apprenticed not to one of the

famous painters who were then living in Seville, but to
an image-maker of so little repute that nothing is known
of him but that he was Zurbaran's master. I should have
thought the explanation was simple. It is true that the
image-makers were often painters as well. Alonso Cano,
for instance, was as highly esteemed for his polychrome
statues as for his paintings, and though Pedro Diaz de
Villanueva was chiefly occupied in carving the images,
large and small, which were not only placed in churches
but were also sought after by the laity for their private
devotions, it is likely enough that he painted pictures;
but if so, not one has survived. Francisco de Herrera,
Juan del Castillo and Juan de las Roelas, who had studied
with Titian, were at this time well-known teachers in
Seville, and their paintings were highly thought of; it is
not unreasonable to suppose that they would have refused
to take a pupil for the modest sum Zurbaran's peasant
father was prepared to pay. If he apprenticed the boy to an
insignificant artisan it is surely because he was cheap.

The most interesting thing we know about the three
years of Zurbaran's apprenticeship is that he became
friends with Velasquez, who was studying with Herrera
el Viejo. For long the influence of the Italian schools
had been paramount in Spain, but about this time the
paintings of Ribera began to be known, and because
they appealed to marked idiosyncrasies of the Spanish
character grew popular. Ribera was a Spaniard, but at an
early age, after studying for some time with Ribalta at
Valencia, he made his way to Rome. There he worked
with Caravaggio, the head of the naturalistic school and
a master of chiaroscuro. The violent contrasts of light and
shade, the dramatic power, the sombre tones with which
Ribera painted gruesome scenes of martyrdom were very
much to the taste not only of the public, but also of the
young painters who were impatient of the conventionality
of masters who were still practising an art that had lost
its savour. So great, indeed, was Ribera's influence on

the young Velasquez and on the young Zurbaran that several of their early pictures have at various times been ascribed first to one and then to the other. For example, the *Adoration of the Shepherds* in the National Gallery, long considered to be by Velasquez, is now attributed to Zurbaran.

The Church frowned on the use in schools of the nude model, so the student, as exercises to prepare himself to paint the human figure, which was then the artist's only subject-matter, painted still-lifes and flower-pieces, but anything of the kind Zurbaran may have produced during this period has perished, and his first extant painting is an Immaculate Conception dated 1616. He was then eighteen. It is a hard, careful portrait of a young girl standing in space on the heads of eight cherubs, and it owes its composition very obviously to Italian influence. At about the same time he must have painted the *Virgin as a Child in Prayer*, for he has used the same homely, fat-faced wench as a model.

II

Zurbaran lived obscurely, and little can be told of him that is more than conjecture. That is not to be wondered at, for there is of necessity a great deal of monotonous regularity in a painter's life. His occupation is physically exhausting, and after his day's work is done he is unlikely to have much inclination to indulge in the kind of adventures that provide matter for a biographer. In Zurbaran's time a painter did not, as now, paint pictures because he had a mind to and trust to finding a patron to buy them; he had no money to buy colours and canvases, the appurtenances of his art, and painted on commission. His social position was humble, on a level with the goldsmith's and silversmith's, the cabinet-maker's and the bookbinder's. He was a craftsman who led a modest and straitened life, and no one thought it worth his while to record its vicissitudes. If he had love-affairs they were no one's business but his own, and his comings and goings were of little interest to anyone but himself. But when an artist has won fame the world is curious to know what sort of man he was; it is hard to believe that someone who has produced work of a rare and original quality should have been to all seeming a very ordinary person whose life was no more exciting than a bank-clerk's. It happens then that legends arise and though there is no evidence for them they may so accord with the instinctive impression his work furnishes, or, if there are portraits of him, with the look of him, as to have a certain plausibility.

So it has happened with Zurbaran. The story goes that before he left Fuente de Cantos, never to return, he drew a vicious caricature of a gentleman of property who lived there. This gentleman, named Silverio de Luerca, on hearing of it, went to the boy's house and asked for him. His father told him that he had gone away, but refused to say where he was, upon which the incensed young man hit him so violent a blow on the head that within five days he died of it. Luerca fled to Madrid, where owing to influential friends he escaped the consequences of his crime, and in course of time came to occupy posts of some importance under Philip IV. Many years passed. Zurbaran went to Madrid, either because he had work to do there or because he was looking for work, and one night on his way home he came across two men who were taking leave of one another. One said: 'Good night, Luerca, see you tomorrow'; and walked away. Zurbaran went up to the man who had been thus addressed and asked him: 'Are you by chance Don Silverio de Luerca, a native of Fuente de Cantos?'

'I am.'

'Then draw your sword, for the blood of my father cries out for blood, and his life demands yours. I am Francisco de Zurbaran.'

They fought. The conflict was brief. Silverio de Luerca fell to the ground crying: 'I am a dead man,' and Zurbaran fled from the scene.

The story is certainly characteristic of the period, when the point of honour was an obsession with the Spaniards and everyone, not only gentlemen and soldiers, but haberdashers and lackeys, carried a sword and was quick to resent affront. There is in the gallery at Brunswick a portrait, said to be of Zurbaran, which gives a certain likelihood to the legend. It is that of a man of a swarthy complexion, with a head of untidy black hair, a black moustache and a black goatee, dark eyes and a stern, harsh look. You would not have said that this was a man to forget or to forgive an injury. There is in Madrid a drawing which is also presumed to be a portrait of Zurbaran, but when he was much older. The hair is thin and white, the expression mild. In neither case, however, are there better grounds for the ascription than that it has for a long time been made. He is said to have painted himself in one or other of his large compositions, in the great *Apotheosis of St. Thomas Aquinas*, for instance, and in the picture at Guadalupe of Henry III offering a bishopric to the prior. This again is mere guess-work.

But there is a small picture, recently acquired by the Prado, which one must be of a very sceptical temper not to accept as an authentic portrait of the artist in his old age. It is entitled *Jesus Christ with St. Luke in the guise of a painter*. Christ is on the Cross, and standing by his side, with a palette on his thumb and brushes in his fingers, is a painter. He is thin and worn, with a great Adam's apple protruding from his skinny neck, bald except at the back of his head, from which lank grey locks hang to his shoulders. He has the same high cheek-bones as in the Brunswick picture, but the cheeks are sunken; he has a bold, hooked nose, a long upper lip and a somewhat receding chin partly concealed by a sparse and straggling beard. He wears a loose brown smock such as Zurbaran or any painter today might wear to paint in. It is the portrait of a man broken by the years, by poverty, neglect and disappointment. His right hand is pressed to his heart and he looks up at his dying Lord with the humble, pathetic adoration of a dog unjustly beaten.

After finishing his apprenticeship Zurbaran seems to have gone to Llerena, a prosperous town in Estremadura not far from his birthplace, and there, according to Doña Maria Luisa Caturla, who has spent laborious years in a study of the artist's life and works, he married a certain Maria Paez. Her father had a large family and was by calling a gelder. Zurbaran was then eighteen and his wife some years older. Since the marriage brought him neither cash nor credit it must be supposed that it was a love match. A son was born to the couple in 1620 and a daughter in 1623. Maria Paez appears to have died about then, perhaps in childbirth, and in 1625 Zurbaran married Beatriz de Morales, a widow, who was a native of Llerena, and, again according to Doña Maria Luisa Caturla, hard on forty years of age. It is curious that he should twice have married women much older than himself. Beatriz de Morales bore him a daughter. She died in 1639 and five years later he married Doña Leonor de Tordesas, a widow of twenty-eight and the daughter of a goldsmith. By her he had no less than six children.

Strangely enough, with the exception of the two pictures I have mentioned, there is no trace of any of Zurbaran's paintings for something like eight years after he went to Llerena; yet he must have been slowly acquiring a reputation, for in 1624 he was commissioned to execute nine large compositions dealing with the life of St. Peter for the cathedral of Seville. This done, he went back to Llerena and is supposed to have spent two or three years more there; he was then invited by the monks of a convent in Seville to return to the city to paint for their new cloister a series of pictures concerned with the life of

St. Peter Nolasco. He agreed to do this and after finishing his task he painted a Crucifixion for the convent of St. Paul. These works excited so much admiration that a petition was presented to the town council by certain gentlemen praying that 'in view of the consummate art he had shown in these productions, and taking for granted that painting is not the least ornament of the state,' he should be solicited to take up his residence in Seville, 'if not on a salary or with a contribution to his expenses, at least in language that would gratify him, since such an approach would effect the purpose.' The town council, having considered the matter, charged the author of the petition, Don Rodrigo Suarez, to inform Zurbaran 'how much the city desired that he should dwell there on account of the favourable opinions they had formed of him, and the city would take care to favour him, and to assist him on all occasions that presented themselves.' Zurbaran accepted the flattering invitation and, as a statement he made later indicates, sent to Llerena for his wife and children.

But this was not the end of the matter. The local painters were incensed that one whom, since he came from Estremadura, they looked upon as a foreigner should be settled among them in such an honourable way. Since for the most part the only commissions to be secured were to paint for churches and convents, the market was limited, and the competition of a stranger was resented. Alonso Cano presented another petition to the council protesting against the resolution they had passed and calling upon them to have Zurbaran interrogated to determine his qualifications. The town council seem to have been strangely amenable to petitions, for they agreed that what Alonso Cano asked was reasonable, and to Zurbaran's indignation the heads of the painters' union (for so I translate *alcaldes pintores*), supported by other members of the craft, with a scrivener and a policeman to accredit their authority, forthwith went to inform him that he must within three days submit to examination.

53

He immediately called the council's attention to the fact that they themselves had invited him to stay in Seville on account of his eminence as a painter and for the glory of the city, whereupon at great personal inconvenience he had transferred his residence from Llerena to Seville, and he requested them therefore to declare that he was under no obligation to comply with so insulting a demand. It may be presumed that the town council saw the justice of his claim, for he remained in Seville, and continued to execute the numerous commissions he received from all parts of the peninsula.

In 1634 he was bidden to Madrid by Velasquez at the order of Philip IV to paint pictures for the palace called El Buen Retiro which the favourite, the Count-Duke of Olivares, was building to divert the King's attention from the unhappy condition of the country and the disastrous wars with Holland, France and England, for all of which the obstinate folly of the Count-Duke was responsible. Velasquez had been settled in Madrid for some years. At that time if an artist did not paint religious pictures he could only make a living by painting portraits, and since such money as there was in Spain was to be found at Court, it was by repairing thither that the portrait-painter was most likely to meet with patrons. It is possible that Velasquez was unable to get commissions for religious pictures in his birthplace, where, as is shown by the efforts made by the painters of Seville to drive Zurbaran from the city, the competition was keen, or it may be that his astute father-in-law, Pacheco, saw that his great gifts would better serve him in Madrid; the fact remains that he went there, and there, as we know, he soon gained the King's favour and so entered upon his triumphal career. The commission offered to Zurbaran was to paint a series of canvases illustrating the labours of Hercules. I shall have something to say about them later; here I will only relate a charming anecdote that has come down to us. He had been given the honorary title of the King's Painter, either for the work he was then engaged on or for the decoration of a boat which the nobles of Seville had presented to Philip so that he might take his ease in it on the placid waters of the pleasure-grounds which surrounded his new palace. One day, having finished one of these pictures, he affixed his signature: Francisco de Zurbaran, the King's Painter. Someone touched him on the shoulder. He turned round and saw a gentleman in black standing behind him, a gentleman with long fair hair, a long pale face, pale blue eyes, and a long chin. It was the King. With a smile His Majesty of Spain, with the courtesy for which he was famous, pointed to the signature and said: 'The King's Painter and the Painters' King.'

The compliment was gracious, but does not appear to have been followed by the offer of further employment, for when Zurbaran had executed this commission he returned to Seville. He painted then for the Charterhouse at Jerez de la Frontera the fine pictures which are now in the museum at Cadiz. In 1638 he went to Guadalupe. Of the work he did there I shall also have something to say presently.

Zurbaran was paid small sums for his paintings and with a large family to support he can have had little chance to save money. Merely to pay his way he needed constant orders. The artist depends on the favour of the public. He spends years learning his craft and developing the personality which will give the peculiar tang to his work which is his originality; and it may be long then before he assembles a sufficient number of patrons to provide him with means adequate to his needs. But too often it happens that though he is still in full possession of his talent a younger man appears on the scene who has something new to offer which, even if inferior in quality, by the attraction of its novelty captures the fickle fancy of the public. What pleased before pleases no longer. This is what befell Zurbaran. People grew tired of the sort of pictures he painted and turned eagerly to the productions of a man still in his twenties who was supplying them with something that appealed to their emotions as perhaps the honest, sober work of Zurbaran had never done – Murillo. He was facile and graceful, his colour was rich and harmonious, and about the time of Zurbaran's third marriage, when he had adopted what is known as his 'warm' style, he was the most popular painter in Seville. He combined realism with sentimentality and so responded to two marked traits of the Spanish character. Zurbaran received fewer and fewer commissions. He does not seem to have signed a single picture between 1639 and 1659 and one can only suppose that if he painted any he did not think them important enough to affix his signature to them. In 1651 he went once more to Madrid, perhaps to see Velasquez, who had just returned from his second visit to Italy, and through whose influence, it may be, he hoped to get another commission from the King; but if this was his object, he failed, and shortly afterwards he went back to Seville. Things seem to have gone from bad to worse, for in 1656, because he had not paid the rent of his house for a year, his effects were seized and put up at auction; but so wretched were they that not a single bid was made.

Two years later he went to Madrid again, but this time for good, and so far as anyone knows he spent the rest of his life there. He was then sixty. He was old to attempt a new manner. Such communication as an artist has to make is primarily to his contemporaries. He may have curious and unusual things to tell them, but he speaks to them in the idiom of his day. Another generation adopts another idiom. There is one thing that is fairly certain, an artist can only develop on the lines which nature has marked out for him, his mode of expression is of the essence of his personality and the attempt to assume a new one is futile. If the language he speaks is no longer understood he must be content to remain silent and trust to the amends which time may have in store for him. Time sifts the significant from the trivial. Posterity is unconcerned with the fashions of a bygone era; it chooses from the mass of material that has come down it what responds to its immediate needs.

But Zurbaran had to live, and to live he had to paint the sort of pictures people wanted. They wanted the sort of pictures that Murillo painted. This is what Zurbaran set himself to do. It was an unfortunate experiment. The pictures he painted had little of his own strength and none of Murillo's charm.

He was still alive in 1664, for in that year he was engaged as an expert to decide the value of a collection of pictures, fifty-five in all, after the death of their owner, a certain Don Francisco Jacinto de Salcedo. It is perhaps significant of the conditions which then prevailed that on the list that has come down to us the names of the painters are not given, but only the subjects and the dimensions of the canvases. The highest value was put upon the largest. It represented the Adoration of the Kings and was ten foot long and just under eight foot high. It was valued at fifteen hundred reals. The real, according to Cotgrave, was equivalent to the English sixpence; so that, including the frame, which was then apt to be elaborate, highly decorated and costly, the picture was estimated to be worth thirty-seven pounds, ten shillings. The average value of full-length portraits of saints and monks seems to have been about five hundred reals, which was fifteen pounds. It is no wonder, if such were the prices paid, that Zurbaran was reduced to penury, and Murillo, his successful rival, died without leaving enough money for his burial.

III

Velasquez died before Zurbaran and in his place other artists were officially created Painters to the King, Mazo first and then Carreño. The dynasty of the Hapsburgs came to an end, and with the Bourbons the eighteenth century entered Spain. Zurbaran's art had nothing to say to a public that admired Van Loo and his sons, Rafael Mengs and Tiepolo. The nineteenth century knew nothing of him, and it was not till certain historical events occurred that his own countrymen thought to remember him. After the disasters of the Spanish-American war in which Spain lost the last remnants of the great empire upon which, Charles V could boast, the sun never set, the Spaniards, humiliated by the crushing defeat, sought by looking back on the glories of their Golden Age to find something in which they could still take pride. Cuba and the Philippines had gone, but nothing could rob them of the magnificence of their cathedrals and palaces, the genius of their writers Cervantes, Lope de Vega, Calderon, Quevedo, and the splendour of their painters.

Velasquez was already world-famous, and the discerning throughout Europe after some hesitation were succumbing to the enigmatic lure of El Greco, but it was left to the Spaniards themselves to rescue Zurbaran from oblivion. And when at last they took cognisance of him I think they must have felt, as we may all feel now, that he was the most Spanish of the three. He lacked the dazzling, air-fraught brilliance of Velasquez, the passionate intensity of El Greco, but he was of the soil as was neither of the others. He had the qualities which the Spaniards recognised in themselves. He had the honesty, the sobriety, the deep religious feeling, the self-respect, the hardihood, which, notwithstanding the misrule of three centuries, the profligacy of courts, the amiable frivolity of the eighteenth century, the dull stupidity of the nineteenth, they felt were deep-rooted in their being. His want of imagination did not offend them, for they were not creatures of ardent imagination, and his realism was agreeable to them, for they were inveterately realistic. They were not romantic, for romance is more at home in the misty north and thrives ill under a southern sun, but they were passionate, and in Zurbaran's pictures they dimly felt a passion held in check by force of will and by self-respect.

In 1905 the Spaniards collected as many of his pictures as they could procure and gave an exhibition of them in the Prado. I do not know what impression it made on the public; I cannot discover that it made any on the rest of Europe.

The paintings Zurbaran did for the Buen Retiro have been an embarrassment to his admirers, and for long they threw doubt on their authenticity, but that persevering searcher of the archives, Doña Maria Luisa Caturla, has within the last few years discovered a receipt for them signed by Zurbaran. They are poor. The subject doubtless was ungrateful, and it may be that it could only have been treated, as for example Piero da Cosimo might have treated it, with fantasy, as a decoration enlivened by little fauns disporting on the green, gaily coloured birds and mythological animals; but such a treatment could scarcely have occurred to Zurbaran. He was of a literal disposition. There was no place in his earnest realism for caprice. There is nothing heroic in his Hercules, nothing to remind you that he was the son of a god and of a princess of Mycenæ; he is but a Spanish peasant, naked but for a loin-cloth, muscular, coarse and ill-favoured; he might be no more than a professional strong man in a fair. The industrious lady performed an equivocal service to Zurbaran when she proved beyond question that he was their author.

But an artist has the right to be judged by his best work. This he generally produces within a comparatively few years; with Zurbaran this seems to have lasted from 1626 to 1639. Now, the *Labours of Hercules* were painted in 1634, when he was at the height of his powers. What is the explanation? The only one I can suggest is that like every other artist Zurbaran had his limitations, and when he attempted something out of their compass he could fail worse than one with lesser gifts would have done. I think he was a modest, sensible man, and he was accustomed to carry out the wishes of his patrons; one cannot suppose that, even if he had been able to afford it, the thought of refusing a royal commission crossed his mind. He was given a job to do, and he did it to the best of his ability. In this case he made a mess of it. There can be little doubt that the instructions which his ecclesiastical patrons gave him were precise, and he was obliged to follow them. Though they ordered pictures to adorn chapels, churches and sacristies, their aim primarily was not to acquire a work of art, but a work of edification, and also, and this frequently, one that should serve to glorify the community that had commissioned it by portraying for the devout and generous public its eminent members, the miracles they had performed, the graces of which they had been the recipients, and even the martyrdom one or other of them had suffered. On occasion their demands rendered it impossible for the painter to contrive a satisfactory composition. There is in the Prado a picture of Zurbaran's representing the Vision of St. Peter Nolasco. The Heavenly City, which an angel points out, is inset in the upper left-hand corner with a very disturbing effect. The angel reminds you of a lecturer delivering a travelogue, and you expect him at any moment to give the operator a nod, on which with a jerk the slide will display another aspect of the city.

Zurbaran had no great skill in composition and little ingenuity of invention; he is at his best in single figures or, if he has to deal with more, in very simple arrangements.

What he could do in favourable circumstances one may judge for oneself from the eight huge pictures he painted for the sacristy at Guadalupe. They may be seen in the place they were painted for, and therefore to their best advantage, and one may accept the tradition in the convent that he designed the polychrome frames and advised upon the decoration, somewhat fussy to the taste of today, of the walls and ceiling. They represent notable events in the lives of certain monks of the order. Four are signed by Zurbaran, and four, of less importance, are not, so it has been supposed that, though begun by Zurbaran, they were finished by another hand. It was while he was engaged on this task that his wife contracted the illness from which she died, and it may be that he left it incomplete to be with her at her death.

Common opinion holds that Zurbaran's masterpiece is the *Apotheosis of St. Thomas Aquinas* which is now in the museum at Seville; I should have said rather that his masterpiece was the eight pictures, taken collectively, which I am now considering. They exhibit all his merits and none of his defects. In some of his paintings, in those at Grenoble for instance, his personages are distressingly wooden; they are lay figures, not human beings. The personages of the pictures at Guadalupe are of flesh and blood. They have the animation of life. They are convincingly real. Zurbaran was a very good draughtsman, and he seems to have had something of a dramatic sense which enabled him to arrange the set and choose the properties so as to give verisimilitude to the scene he was depicting. The backgrounds are pleasing, but conventional, and it is evident that his main interest was in the characterisation of his sitter. His models, I may add, were the monks who happened to be in the convent when he was there. One of the most impressive of these productions is the portrait of Father Gonzalo de Illescas, who was prior of the monastery about the middle of the fifteenth century. He is shown at his desk, a pen in his raised hand, looking up as though there had been a knock on the door and he were waiting for someone to come in. The face might be that of any business man of today, thoughtful, able and guarded. As I tried to explain to the reader at the beginning of this essay, such an establishment as Santa Maria de Guadalupe, with its widespread estates, its feudatory towns, its immense herds, with its hospitals and hostels, was a great business undertaking, and the prior, who was during his term of office in absolute control, had to be, though certainly of a piety sufficient to command respect, a very active man of affairs. Zurbaran's colour, though sober, hard, harsh even, and a trifle cold, was sumptuous. Such of the pictures in the sacristy as face the windows have been exposed to the violent light of the Spanish summer for three hundred years and the colour has faded to the soft tints of pastel. This has deprived them something of their force, but for all that there is a nobility about them which is imposing. There is in them the easy power of a craftsman who knows his business.

The *Apotheosis of St. Thomas Aquinas* is of vast dimensions and the figures are more than life-size. St. Thomas is standing on a cloud, with a pen in one hand and an open book in the other, and on each side of him, seated on clouds presumably, are four doctors of the Church magnificently attired. Below, on each side of a column behind which is a charming view of a street, are two kneeling groups, in one of which is the Emperor Charles V with three of his courtiers, and in the other, accompanied by three monks, the archbishop who built the church for the altarpiece of which this huge production was designed. Above, in the clouds, are Jesus Christ, carrying the Cross like a gun, the Blessed Virgin and two other inhabitants of the celestial region who have been identified as St. Paul and St. Dominic. The picture is impressive by its size, the vigour of its execution, the proficiency of its draughtsmanship and the brilliance of its colour; but you cannot fail to notice the awkwardness of its composition. It is divided into three sections so that the eye cannot survey it comfortably as a whole, and the lowest part, which should surely be the least important, is the most attractive. The name of the model who sat for St. Thomas has come down to us. He was a canon of the Cathedral of Seville, Don Augustin Abreu de Escobar, and a friend of Zurbaran's. In portraiture, when the sitter is a person of eminence, it is less necessary that a portrait should resemble him than that people who know him only by hearsay or through his works should feel that that is exactly how he must look. This is even more so when a painter sets out to represent someone who is long since dead. But in his portrayal of St. Thomas Aquinas, Zurbaran has painted a man who can scarcely have resembled him. You cannot persuade yourself that the Seraphic Doctor was a spry, plump young man of undistinguished appearance.

Zurbaran seldom made mistakes like this. There is in the museum at Seville a large picture of Pope Urban II in conference with St. Bruno. St. Bruno was the founder of the Carthusian order and was come to Rome from his retreat in the valley of the Chartreuse at the request of Urban II. Zurbaran has caught with his accustomed skill the characteristics of the Pope, who was a temporal as well as a spiritual ruler, and of the ascetic monk. Bruno is looking down, his hands modestly concealed in the sleeves of his habit. His face is emaciated, and there is in the expression, notwithstanding the humility of his bearing, the strength of purpose, the obstinacy with which according to history he fought simony and corruption in the Church. The Pope looks out at the spectator with a hard, shrewd look, a man accustomed to command and accustomed to be obeyed, but yet with a certain anxiety in his expression, as though, face to face with this austere, obdurate monk, whose pupil he had been, he did not, for all his great station, feel quite sure of himself.

At about the same time that Zurbaran painted this fine picture he painted for the same convent a picture representing St. Hugo, Bishop of Grenoble, visiting the convent which with his assistance St. Bruno had founded. The seven monks who constituted the new order are seated at their meal in the refectory. The white habits, which Zurbaran painted so admirably, have a curious stiffness. This is said to be due to the fact that whereas Zurbaran painted the heads from nature, he painted the clothes from lay figures. It is an old tradition; but I cannot see why, though he disposed the habits on a lay figure, they should not have hung in natural folds; it seems more plausible that if in many of his pictures the habits hang in folds that no material could assume, so that they appear to be of cardboard (as for example in the St. Antony with the Infant Jesus), it is owing to his early training as a wood-carver with the *imaginero* who was his master. He never quite lost his fondness for the stylised folds of material. It is, indeed, a fine simplification which gave him opportunity for the chiaroscuro in which he delighted, and to my mind it gives a dramatic value to the figures of many of the innumerable monks he painted.

When I said that Zurbaran lacked imagination I exaggerated; it would have been more accurate to say that he lacked fancy. Portraiture, and Zurbaran was pre-eminently a painter of portraits, is to some extent a collaboration between the painter and his sitter; the sitter must give something; there must be something in him which excites the painter's sensibility sufficiently to enable him to portray somewhat more than his model's outward seeming. The painter must have a faculty resembling the novelist's by virtue of which he can slip into the skin of the characters he creates and think their thoughts and feel their feelings. This faculty is imagination and this Zurbaran possessed. His sitters are so sharply individualised that it requires little perspicacity to discern their dispositions and idiosyncrasies. In the great array of his monkish portraits Zurbaran has depicted most of the humours to which men are prone. In this array you may recognise in turn the idealist, the mystic, the saint; the fanatic, the stoic, the autocrat, the precisian; the self-seeker, the sensualist, the glutton and the clown. For it was not only the love of God that induced these men to adopt the life of a religious. Sometimes it was frustrated ambition or a disappointment in love, sometimes a longing for peace and security and sometimes a desire, natural enough, to rise in the world, since if he was not inclined to seek fortune in America or in the wars, the Church offered the only means whereby a poor but clever boy of humble origins could hope to achieve distinction.

Zurbaran painted few secular portraits of men, but on the other hand many of young women, mostly beautiful, and dressed in the handsome clothes of the period. Since the young do not in the general cast of their features often display character he was unable to exhibit his peculiar gift for characterisation, and since the young women of his day, like those of ours, smothered their faces with paint and powder, thereby making themselves look as much like one another as they could, he satisfied himself with giving them good looks, and painting with a wealth of colour the silks and satins of their dress, their pearls and jewelled brooches. Of those I have seen the most striking is that of Santa Casilda. It is in the Prado. She has little of the youthful charm that marks the others, but a face in which there is, with a certain homeliness, an air of the somewhat severe distinction which we are apt to call aristocratic.

The interesting thing about these female portraits is that they purport to represent saints, but if you trouble to look into the lives of the various persons named you discover that, saintly as they were, they could never have worn such gorgeous clothes nor possessed such costly ornaments. There is evidence that at the period during which Zurbaran was active a fashion arose in Spain to have portraits painted either of the daughters or wives of noblemen, or by gentlemen of the objects of their affection, with the attributes of certain saints. Lope de Vega had a lady, with whom, from what we know of him, we may guess his relations were far from continent, painted as the Chaste Susanna, and it is recorded that a Prince of Esquilache caused his mistress to be portrayed with the insignia and in the costume of St. Helena. These saints of Zurbaran were the ladies of Seville. Spanish women of position, owing to the Moorish influence still in some respects prevalent, lived in seclusion, and it seems to have been thought unbecoming, unless they were of the blood royal, that they should allow themselves to be painted as themselves; but by the exercise of this ingenious subterfuge they managed without offence to their delicacy to gratify a natural desire and by presenting their likeness to church or convent at the same time perform an act of piety. It can hardly have failed to be a source of satisfaction when they attended Mass in the chapel of their predilection to see a picture of themselves hanging on a wall or decorating an altarpiece. There were no private views of the Royal Academy nor *vernissages* at the Salon, to which they could go to hear the comments of all and sundry on the portrait that hung on the line; but we may surmise that it was with just such a mingling of pride and apprehension as obtains today that these ladies listened to the congratulations of their friends who came to the chapel to see, to admire, to criticise, to decry the picture of their intimate acquaintance as St. Agnes, St. Rufina or St. Marina.

In speaking of the paintings of Zurbaran I have mentioned his masterly draughtsmanship, the felicity, the variety, the depth of tone with which he represented the white of his monks' habits, the opulence of colour in the habiliments of princes of the Church and the dresses of great ladies; I have dwelt on the sincerity of his workmanship, his honest craftsmanship, his dignity, his sobriety; and I have laid stress on his convincing portraiture, his keen appreciation of character and the persuasiveness of his representation of persons long since dead; I have pointed out how impressive these huge canvases are and how on occasion they have a striking nobility. I cannot expect the reader to have noticed that I have not claimed that any of the pictures I have spoken of had beauty. Beauty is a grave word. It is a word of high import. It is used lightly now – of the weather, of a smile, of a frock or the fit of a shoe, of a bracelet, of a garden, of a syllogism; beautiful serves as a synonym for good or pretty or pleasing or nice or engaging or interesting. But beauty is none of these. It is much more. It is very rare. It is a force. It is an enravishment. It is not a figure of speech when people say it takes their breath away; in certain cases it may give you the same suffocating shock as when you dive into ice-cold water. And after that first shock your heart throbs like a prisoner's when the jail gate clangs behind him and he breathes again the clean air of freedom. The impact of beauty is to make you feel greater than you are, so that for a moment you seem to walk on air; and the exhilaration and the release are such that nothing in the world matters any more. You are wrenched out of yourself into a world of pure spirit. It is like falling in love. It *is* falling in love. It is an ecstasy matching the ecstasy of the mystics. When I think of the works of art that have filled me with this intense emotion I think of the first glance at the Taj Mahal, the St. Maurice of El Greco, seen again after long years, the Adam with his outstretched arm in the Sistine Chapel, Night and Day and the brooding figure of Giuliano on the tombs of the Medici and Titian's *Entombment of Christ*. Such an emotion I, for my part, have never received from the highly competent, well-painted, well-drawn, dignified, thoughtful canvases which Zurbaran painted for the altars of churches and the sacristies of convents. They have great qualities, but they appeal to the mind, to the intelligent appreciation, rather than to the heart and nerves which are thrilled and shattered by the rapture of pure beauty.

Yet he did paint a few pictures, in size or importance of subject of no great consequence, which to my mind have a rare and moving beauty, and of these I propose presently to speak. But before I do this I must deal with another topic.

When the Spaniards re-discovered Zurbaran and hailed him as one of the glories of their country they claimed that he was a mystical painter. Nothing could be further from the truth, and it is to the great credit of Don Bernardino de Pantorba, author of a very sensible, though too brief, essay on Zurbaran, that he has pointed out how mistaken they were. It is true that for the most part he painted pictures of religious subjects; as I have pointed out, Churchmen were his chief patrons, and there can be little doubt that this serious, simple-minded man was a good Catholic. The Spaniards have always been of a religious turn – after their fashion, and in the seventeenth century they were intensely devout. The Council of Trent was still fresh in their minds and the Inquisition was alert to punish any suspicion of heresy. But it was a devotion at once fervid, sentimental, grim and brutal. To see to what extravagance it could be carried one need only read Calderon's play, *La Devocion de la Cruz*. We may be pretty sure that Zurbaran performed his religious duties with unction. It has seemed to me that one can get some inkling of the nature of his religion from one of the pictures he painted for the convent at Guadalupe. It represents St. Jerome being chastised by two angels because of his excessive predilection for secular literature. He is on his knees, naked but for a loin-cloth, and the two angels with whips in their hands are belabouring him with might and main, while Jesus Christ sitting on a cloud a little way off, with one hand upraised as though he were counting the strokes, wears an expression of mild complacency. Since it is stated that the Saint's particular transgression was to read the works of Cicero to the neglect of the inspired Word of God, an irreverent person might suggest that he owed this castigation to a rival author's annoyance that another author's works should be read as well as, or in competition with, his own. But the significant thing is that the Saint is evidently deeply conscious of his sin, and his attitude of supplication indicates not only that he prays for forgiveness, but looks upon the hiding he receives as well-deserved. I think we may hazard the surmise that Zurbaran thought so too.

In his various representations of Christ Zurbaran surrendered to a sentimentality that was alien to his temperament. He gives him the offensive smugness of the self-satisfied rector of a fashionable church. This is not the compassionate yet stern and virile teacher who delivered the Sermon on the Mount. But on the other hand his Crucifixions display a sombre power that was all his own. He does nothing to palliate the horror of the tragic scene. A dark and stormy background emphasises the solitude of the sufferer. In one, with the head downcast, the face in deep shadow, there is, strangely, a moving expression of despair. The body has already the cold greyness of a corpse. In another the agony of the uplifted face, appealing, you would have said in vain, to a deaf God has a harrowing intensity. It could hardly have failed to exacerbate the emotions of a people who found such a dreadful fascination in the spectacle of their Saviour's anguish.

It may be that Zurbaran's religious pictures accorded with the religious conception of the Spaniards of his day and aroused the feelings of devotion which they were designed to do. I don't think they can do that now. I have a notion that by his time faith had been rendered too formal, too rigid, too chartered for a painter to feel, and so portray, the artless emotion which makes the works of the early Sienese painters so simply and naïvely religious. The observances of religion were a method by which you escaped the tortures of hell and won the reward of eternal bliss, and your spiritual advisers were there with their cut-and-dried rules to point out your way for you and, if necessary, to indicate a short cut.

And of course it is a mistake to suppose that mysticism is necessarily religious in character. The mystic experience is a specific thing. It is true that it may arise from the practice of religion, and then it is generally the reward of prayer and mortification, but it may also arise through the influence of a drug, opium, for instance, or the mescal bean, and in rare instances from the hypnotic suggestion of running water (as with St. Ignatius Loyola), and sometimes from the impact of beauty on a soul of peculiar sensibility. So many people have described in terms so similar the ecstasy of illumination that there can be little doubt of its reality. I do not know that they who experience it through the effects of a drug or the impact of beauty draw the same inferences as do they who experience it through the practice of religion, but the sensations are the same, a sense of liberation, a sense that they are united with something larger than themselves, a sense of exhilaration, a sense of awe and of detachment from all that is base, idle and transitory.

Is it rash to suggest that when the artist, poet or painter, is mysteriously seized with that curious humour which is known as inspiration, so that notions come to him he cannot tell whence and he finds himself aware of things he never knew he knew, he enjoys a condition indistinguishable from that of the mystic in rapture?

It is absurd to call Zurbaran a mystic. He was, as a matter of fact, a downright, literal fellow, who was given a job to do and did it as well as he could. It is true that, like other painters of religious subjects, he painted various saints and monks in ecstasy. But he used the common formula. He painted them with their mouths gaping and their eyes turned up towards heaven so that little is seen but their whites. You are disconcertingly reminded of a dead codfish on a fishmonger's marble slab. The mystical state is probably something that the painter cannot represent, and it is not by attempting to do so that he can arouse in the spectator the mystical emotion which art can sometimes induce. I have seemed myself to feel it when I have contemplated the painting of the flesh in El Greco's *Crucifixion* in the Louvre and in one or two of Chardin's still-lifes. It is quite a different feeling from that which you get from the ingenuous and heart-felt pictures of the Sienese Primitives. Kant, as we all know, claimed that the sublime does not exist in nature, but is introduced into it by the sensibility of men of a considerable degree of culture. So it may be that mysticity does not reside in pictures, but that some pictures have in them a potentiality which enables a beholder of a peculiar disposition, of some aesthetic training, to infuse them with a magic which excites in him the mystical experience. They have then a beauty deeper than the beauty which takes your breath away, they have a beauty which is tremulous and animating so that for a brief moment you experience the same ecstasy as the saints experience in communion with Divine Reality.

I have spoken of Zurbaran as though he were a plodding, industrious, competent painter who painted pictures as a cabinet-maker might make a *bargueño* or a potter turn out an Hispano-Moorish plate. And so he was. He was no genius. And yet, perhaps because he was so honest, so sincere, because he had the sensibility which enabled him to paint the white of his monks' habits with such an admirable subtlety, sometimes, very rarely, he was able to surpass his limitations. Sometimes he excelled himself. Not in those huge canvases with their figures life-size or over, not in those representations of miracles or in those portraits of noble ladies masquerading as saints, but in certain small pictures which, when you survey his many works, you may easily overlook. There are in the museum at Cadiz pictures of Carthusian monks, one of St. Bruno, another of the Blessed John Houghton, which are of such beauty, which have in them so much emotion, that you feel that here at all events he was inspired. Of these to my mind the most moving is that of the English Carthusian. I have written about this picture before and I can only repeat what I have already written. I cannot but believe that it was an English monk and not a Spanish one who served Zurbaran as a model, and I have asked myself idly who was this unknown compatriot of mine who sat to the painter for a portrait of another Englishman. There is here the well-bred refinement, the clean-cut, shapely features that you sometimes find in a certain sort of Englishman of gentle birth. The hair, the little of it that is left round the shaven skull, appears to be of a reddish-brown; the face, emaciated from long fasting, has a tension that is restless and eager. A hectic flush mantles the cheek. The skin is darker than ivory, though with the warmly supple hue of ivory, and paler than olive, yet with something of that colour's morbid delicacy. Round his neck, fastened by a knot, is a rope. One wasted hand is clasped to his breast and in the other he holds a bleeding heart.

I have had the curiosity to learn who this beatified monk was, and this is what I have found out. He was born of an ancient family in Essex about 1488. After his education had run its course his parents arranged a marriage for him suitable to his condition, but, determined to embrace a state of celibacy and to dedicate himself to the service of God alone, he secretly left his father's house and hid himself in the house of a devout cleric. There he stayed till he was ordained. For four years after this he exercised the functions of a parish priest. But at the age of twenty-eight, aspiring to a way of life still more perfect, he entered the Carthusian order. In 1530 he was chosen to be prior of the Charterhouse in London. Three years later Anne Boleyn was crowned Queen of England, and John Houghton was required by the Royal Commissioners to declare that Henry's marriage with Catherine of Aragon was invalid. He refused and was sent to the Tower. A somewhat casuistical compromise was effected and he was released; but in the following year a subservient parliament enacted that the King was supreme head on earth of the Church of England, and pronounced every person who repudiated the statute to be a traitor. John Houghton, with two of his brother-priors, refused to take the oath which acknowledged its validity and the three of them were indicted for high treason. The jury hesitated to condemn such holy men as malefactors, but were compelled by Cromwell, the King's Vicar, to bring in a verdict of guilty. They were sentenced to be hanged and quartered. John Houghton ascended the scaffold first. A thick rope was placed round his neck which it was thought would not produce strangulation so quickly as a thin one. He addressed the populace and the ladder was dragged from under him. The rope was cut while he was still alive, and he fell to the ground. They dragged him away from the scaffold, stripped him of his clothes, and his heart and entrails were torn from his body and thrown into the fire.

No one can know whether Zurbaran was unwontedly moved by the pathos of this story or whether there was some characteristic in the model he chose that peculiarly appealed to him: when he painted this young monk, by some happy accident he achieved beauty. On this occasion he was no longer the sensible, level-headed, practical craftsman, but a great painter. On this occasion, inspired, he painted a picture in which there is the mystical exaltation which throbs through the lovely verse of St. John of the Cross.

But it was not alone then that he reached a height you would never have expected him to attain. I mentioned earlier that in his student days Zurbaran, forbidden to work from the nude, is presumed to have painted a number of still-lifes. They have disappeared. But it is plain that throughout he held in peculiar affection the inanimate objects which constitute the subject-matter of still-life. In the picture of St. Hugo visiting the Carthusian monks in their refectory, for instance, the loaves of bread on the table, the bowls containing their food, the earthen-ware jars for the water are painted with an intimacy so sensitive, with an insight so penetrating, that they appear to symbolise something other than themselves.

Now and then, perhaps as a change or a rest, Zurbaran painted a still-life. There is one in the Prado. It shows two bowls and two pitchers in a row on a table against a dark background. The two bowls stand on plates. That is all. It is as simple and straightforward as all Zurbaran's work; yet it is of a staggering beauty. It is as beautiful as the picture of the blessed John Houghton and it fills you with an emotion as intense. One of the things that must strike the sojourner in Spain is the tenderness with which the Spaniards use children. However tiresome they are, however intrusive, wilful, noisy, they seem never to lose patience with them. Well, it seems to me that it is with just this tenderness that Zurbaran painted these modest household utensils. It renders them wonderfully touching. It gives them indeed the same mystical quality which, if you but have the temper to see it, pervades the pictures of those monks at Cadiz. It is for these pictures, for this still-life, for the Christ Crucified, with the painter, old, worn and haggard, looking up at his Saviour that I think one can claim Zurbaran to be a master.

Perhaps that is not very much when you think of his vast production. It is enough. The artist has no need to carry heavy baggage to find his way to posterity. A few pictures, a book or two, suffice. The artist's function is to create beauty, though not, I believe, the mainspring of his productiveness, and not, as some think, to reveal truth: if it were, a syllogism would be more significant than a sonnet. But it is not often that the artist can do more than suggest it or approximate to it, and the layman should be satisfied if he can attain the agreeable. It is only by a rare combination of technique, deep feeling and good fortune that the artist, be he painter or poet, can achieve that beauty which in its effects is akin to the ecstasy which the saints won to by prayer and mortification. Then his poems or his pictures give the sense of deliverance, the exaltation, the happiness, the liberality of spirit which the mystics enjoy in union with the Infinite. To me it is wonderfully moving that Zurbaran, this laborious, honest, matter-of-fact man, should on a few occasions in his long life have been, none can tell why, so transported out of himself as to have done just this. It is as though the grace of God had descended upon him.

The Decline and Fall of the Detective Story

I

When, after a hard day's work, you are spending the evening alone and you look at your bookshelves for something to read, do you take down *War and Peace, L'Education Sentimentale, Middlemarch* or *Du Coté de chez Swann?* If you do I admire you. Or if, wishing to keep up with modern fiction, you take up a novel the publisher has sent you, a harrowing story of displaced persons in Central Europe, or one that a review has induced you to buy, a ruthless picture of the lives of poor white trash in Louisiana, you have my hearty approval. But that is not the sort of person I am. For one thing, I have read all the great novels three or four times already and they have nothing more to tell me; for another, when I look at the four hundred and fifty closely printed pages which according to the jacket are going to lay bare to me the secrets of a woman's soul or wring my withers with the horrors of life in the slums of Glasgow (all the characters speaking broad Scots) my heart sinks; and I choose a detective story.

At the outbreak of the last war I found myself imprisoned at Bandol, a seaside resort on the Riviera, imprisoned, I should add, not by the police but by circumstances. I was in fact in a sailing-boat. She was in peace-time berthed at Villefranche, but the naval authorities ordered us to leave, so we set sail for Marseilles. We were caught in a storm and took refuge at Bandol, where there was something of a harbour. The movements of private individuals were restricted and one could not even go as far as Toulon, but a few miles away, without a permit which could only be obtained after an intolerable delay by filling in a number of forms and producing a number of photographs. I was obliged to stay put.

The summer visitors had fled incontinently and the resort had a surprised and forlorn look. The casino, most of the hotels and many of the shops were closed. The days, however, passed pleasantly enough. There were the *Petit Marseillais* and the *Petit Var* to buy at the stationer's every morning, one's *café au lait* to drink and the marketing to do. I learnt where you could get the best butter for the money and which baker made the best bread. I exerted all my charm to wheedle an old peasant-woman to keep me half a dozen fresh eggs. I found out to my shame that a huge, an enormous mass of spinach had when cooked a very stingy look. I was confounded once more by my ignorance of human nature when I discovered that the keeper of a stall in the market whose honest face attracted my custom had sold me a melon which was too ripe to eat or a camembert (though in a voice tremulous with sincerity she had assured me it was *à point*) which was as hard as a brick. There was always a sporting chance that at ten the English papers would come in, and though they were a week old it was no matter; I read them with eagerness.

At twelve there was the wireless news from Marseilles. Then luncheon and a nap. In the afternoon I walked for exercise up and down the front or stood watching the boys and old men (all the rest had gone) playing their interminable games of *boule*. At five there was the *Soleil* from Marseilles and I read once more what I had read in the morning in the *Petit Marseillais* and the *Petit Var*. After that there was nothing but the wireless news again at half-past seven. At dusk we had to shut ourselves in, and if a chink of light showed, menacing shouts came from the air-wardens who patrolled the quay and we were sternly bidden to screen it. There was nothing to do then but to read detective stories.

With so much leisure it would have been fitting if I had improved my mind by reading one of the great monuments of English literature. I have never read more than a chapter here and there of the *Decline and Fall*, and I have always promised myself that some day I would read it right through from the first page of the first volume to the last page of the last. Here was a heaven-sent opportunity. But life in a forty-five-ton sailing-boat, though sufficiently comfortable, lacks quiet. Next door to the cabin is the galley and there the sailors are cooking their evening meal, with a rattle of pots and pans, and vociferously discussing their private affairs. One of them comes in to fetch a tin of soup or a box of sardines; then he remembers that the motor must be set going or the electricity will fail. Presently the cabin boy clatters down the companion to say he has caught a fish, and will you have it for dinner. Then he comes in to lay the table. The skipper of the boat next to yours gives a hail and a sailor tramps over your head to find out what he wants. The pair have an animated conversation which you cannot help listening to because they both shout at the top of their voices. It is difficult to read with attention. I think it would have been doing an injustice to Gibbon's great work to set about it in such conditions and I must admit that my aloofness of spirit did not extend so far as to have enabled me just then to read it with interest. In fact I should have had difficulty to think of a book I less wanted to read at that time than *The Decline and Fall of the Roman Empire*, and this was lucky because I hadn't got it. On the other hand I had a number of detective stories, which I could always exchange for others belonging to the owners of other boats similarly swinging to their anchors, and there were any number for sale at the stationer's where I bought my papers. During the four weeks I spent at Bandol I read two a day.

This, of course, was not the first occasion on which I had read this class of fiction, but it is the first on which I read it in the mass. Part of the First World War I spent in a sanatorium for the tuberculous in the North of Scotland and there I learnt how pleasant it is to lie in bed, what a delicious sense of liberation it affords from the responsibilities of life and how conducive it is to profitable reflection and aimless reverie. Since then whenever I can square it with my conscience I go to bed. A cold in the head is a distressing ailment for which you get no sympathy. The persons with whom you are brought in contact regard you with anxiety, not because they fear it may turn to pneumonia and result in your demise, but because they fear they will catch it. They scarcely trouble to conceal their irritation that you should expose them to this danger. For my part when thus afflicted I promptly take to my bed. With aspirin, a hot-water bottle, rum toddy at night and half a dozen detective stories I am prepared to make an ambiguous virtue of an equivocal necessity.

I have read hundreds of detective stories, good and bad, and they have to be very bad indeed for me to cast them aside unfinished, but I do not pretend to be more than a dilettante. If I present the reader with the reflections that have occurred to me on this variety of fiction it is with a proper sense of my fallibility.

First of all I should like to distinguish between the shocker and the detective story. I read shockers only by accident, when I have been misled by the title or the wrapper into believing that I was about to engage in a story of crime. They are the bastard descendants of the boys' books, Henty and Ballantyne, which amused our youth, and their vogue is due, one can only suppose, to the fact that there is a large class of adult readers whose minds have remained puerile. I have no patience with these gallant heroes who perform acts of derring-do and those dauntless heroines who after incurring incredible adventures are united to them on the last page. I hate the stiff upper lip of the first and I shudder at the archness of the second. I sometimes wonder idly about their writers. Are they seized with a divine afflatus and do they write because they must with the anguish of spirit with which Flaubert wrote *Madame Bovary*? I refuse to believe that they sit down deliberately to write, tongue in cheek, something that will bring them in a tidy sum of money. If they did I would not blame them, for evidently this is a pleasanter way of earning a living than by selling matches in the street, which exposes you to the inclemency of the weather, or being an attendant in a public lavatory, which affords but a narrow view of human nature. I prefer to think that they are lovers of their species who are deeply moved by the thought of this vast mass of readers that has been created by compulsory education, and by their tales of fire and shipwreck, train accidents, forced landings in the Sahara, smugglers' caves, opium dens, sinister orientals, hope to win their readers to an appreciation of Jane Austen.

It is with the stories of crime that I wish to concern myself, and especially with that of murder. Theft and fraud are crimes too, and they may give rise to some pretty work in detection, but they arouse in me an interest which is no more than languid. From the standpoint of the Absolute, which is the proper standpoint from which to consider this kind of fiction, it does not matter whether the string of pearls that has been stolen is worth twenty thousand pounds or was bought at Woolworth's for a few shillings; and fraud, whether it entails a cool million or three pounds seven and six, is an equally sordid business. The writer of crime stories cannot say like that rather tiresome old Roman that nothing human is alien to him; everything human is alien to him but murder. It is, of course, the most human of crimes, for I suppose we have all at one time or another contemplated it and have been held back from it either from dread of the penalty or from the fear (probably groundless) of our own remorse. But the murderer has taken the risk at which we hesitated and the prospect of the gallows invests his action with a grim impressiveness.

I think authors should be chary of their murders. One is the perfect number, two are permissible, especially when the second is a direct consequence of the first, but it is an unpardonable error to introduce a second murder to enliven an investigation which the author fears is growing tedious. When you have more than two it becomes a massacre and as one violent death follows another you are more inclined to laugh than to quiver. It is a fault of the American authors of crime stories that they are seldom satisfied with one, or even two murders; they shoot, stab, poison or blackjack *en masse*; they are apt to turn their pages into a shambles and the reader is left with the uncomfortable feeling that they have been playing the fool with him. It is a pity, for America with its mixed population and the multifarious cross-currents of its life, with its vitality, ruthlessness and adventurous temper, offers the novelist a far more diverse and inspiring field of action than our own settled, humdrum and on the whole law-abiding country.

II

The theory of the detective story of deduction is simple. Someone is murdered, there is an investigation, suspicion falls on a number of persons, the culprit is discovered and pays the penalty of his crime. This is the classic formula and it contains in itself all the elements of a good story, for it has a beginning, a middle and an end. It was laid down by Edgar Allan Poe in *The Murders in the Rue Morgue* and for many years was scrupulously followed. For long *Trent's Last Case* has been considered the perfect story constructed on these lines. It is written in a more leisurely manner than is now usual, but it is written with an agreeable lightness in good English. The characters are well-drawn and plausible. The humour is unobtrusive. It is a bit of bad luck for Mr. E. C. Bentley that finger-prints, about which at the time he wrote little was known, have now become part of the usual police procedure. They have since then been used by innumerable writers and the elaboration with which Mr. Bentley describes the process has lost its point. Readers of detective stories have now grown crafty, and when a gentle, kindly old man who has apparently no motive to commit a murder is presented to them, they have no hesitation in deciding that it was he who committed it. You cannot read many pages of *Trent's Last Case* without being sure that Mr. Cupples is the guilty party. But you can still read the book with interest to find out why he should have killed Manderson. Mr. Bentley has deliberately neglected to conform to the canon that the crime should be brought home to the culprit by the detective. The mystery would never have been solved if Mr. Cupples had not obligingly revealed the truth. It must be admitted that it is by a most improbable coincidence that he found himself concealed in a place in circumstances which obliged him to shoot Manderson in self-defence. Nor are these circumstances credible. It is asking us to believe too much that a hard-headed business man will plot his own suicide to get his secretary hanged and it is futile to adduce the well-known Campden Case in which John Perry accused his mother, brother and himself of murdering a man, afterwards discovered to be alive, in order to get them hanged even though, as happened, it meant that he would be hanged himself. That something has occurred in real life does not make it a fitting subject of fiction. Life is full of improbabilities which fiction does not admit of.

To me the greatest mystery, never explained, of *Trent's Last Case* is why a man of enormous wealth, with a country house of at least fourteen rooms and an indoor staff of six servants, should have had a garden so small that it needed no more attention than could be given it on two days a week by a man from the village.

But though, as I have said, the theory of the detective story is simple, it is astonishing how many pitfalls beset the author. His aim is to prevent you from discovering who the murderer is till you have reached the end of his book, and he is justified in using every wile he can think of to achieve it. But he must play fair with you. The murderer must be a person who takes a prominent part in the story, and it will not do to make him a shadowy character or one who has figured so slightly that your attention has never been drawn to him. But if he has loomed large in your narrative there is the danger that he will have excited your interest and perhaps your sympathy, so that you will be displeased if he is arrested and put to death. Sympathy is a very ticklish thing. It often attaches itself to a character contrary to the author's intention. (I believe Jane Austen meant Henry and Mary Crawford to be trashy creatures whom the reader was to condemn for their levity and heartlessness, but she has made them so gay and so charming that you like them much better than prim Fanny Price and pompous Edmund Bertram.) There is one curious thing about sympathy which I do not think everyone is aware of. The reader's sympathy goes to those characters who are first presented to him; and not only in crime stories, but in other stories as well, he will be left with the feeling that he has been imposed upon if the persons for whom his interest has been aroused during the first ten pages do not turn out to be those with whom he is afterwards to concern himself. I think it would be worth the while of the writers of detective stories to remember this law and introduce their murderer only after several other characters.

It is evident that if the murderer is from the beginning made odious, with whatever red herrings the ingenious author strews your path, your suspicions will fall on him and the story will be finished before it is begun. Authors sometimes try to evade the quandary by making all or most of the characters odious, so that you have a choice among them. I am not convinced that this is successful. For one thing, it is hard to believe now, as the Victorians did, in unrelieved villainy. We know that people are a mixture of good and bad; we do not believe in them when they are represented as all good or all bad, and as soon as we no longer do that, the author has lost us. We do not care what happens to his puppets. He has got then to make his murderer that same mixture of good and bad that we know human beings are, but he has so to load the dice that when his guilt is brought home to him we are content to see him hanged. One way of loading the dice is to make the crime a very mean and brutal one. Of course we may jib at the notion that such a crime can have been committed by someone who has at least certain engaging traits; but that is the least of the difficulties that here confront the author. No one (in a detective story) has any sympathy for the victim. Either he has been killed before the book starts, or is killed so soon after that, since you know little about him, you can take no interest in him on his own account, his death means no more to you than a chicken's, and however barbarous the method, his decease leaves you cold. Moreover, if suspicion is to be thrown on a number of persons, there must be a number of motives for his murder. He must, by his own crimes, follies, bad temper, brutality, avarice or what not, have made himself so objectionable that his death perturbs you but little. He would presumably not have been killed without good reason, and if we come to the conclusion that he is just as well out of the way we are not too well pleased to see his murderer hanged. Some authors avoid the dilemma by making the murderer commit suicide when he is discovered. This justifies the canon that a life should be paid for a life, but spares the susceptibilities of the reader to whom the circumstances of the hangman's rope are repellent. The murderer then should be bad, but not too bad to be obvious and not too bad to be incredible; his motive should be compelling and he should be sufficiently unsympathetic so that when his crime is brought home to him we should feel that he richly deserves the gallows.

I should like to dwell for a little on this matter of motive. I once visited the penal colony of French Guiana. I have told elsewhere of this experience, but I do not expect anyone to have read all I have written, and since it is to the point I make no apology for repeating myself. There were then at least three establishments to which convicts were sent according to the nature of their crimes and at St. Laurent de Maroni all were murderers. Since the jury had in their verdict allowed that there were extenuating circumstances they had been sentenced not to death, but to a long term of imprisonment. I spent one whole day enquiring into the reasons that had led them to commit their crime. They were quite willing to talk. On the surface many of them seemed to have murdered for love's sake or from jealousy. They had killed their wives, or their wife's lover, or their mistress. But I didn't have to ask much further to discover that the ulterior motive was financial. One man killed his wife because she was spending his money on a lover, another killed his mistress because she stood in the way of his making a rich marriage, a third because she black-mailed him into giving her money by threatening to divulge their relations to his wife. Even when sex had nothing to do with the murder money was still the compelling incentive. One man killed to rob, another killed his brother in a quarrel over the division of an inheritance, a third killed his partner because he did not receive his proper share on the sale of stolen motor-cars. One *apache* killed the woman he was living with because she had betrayed him to the police, another killed a member of a rival gang in revenge for the killing in a drunken brawl of a member of his own gang.

I came across no murder that could justly be described as a crime of passion. Perhaps of course those who had committed one were acquitted by a lenient jury or sentenced to so short a term of imprisonment that they were not sent to Guiana. Another common motive was fear. There was a young shepherd boy who had raped a little girl in a field and when she screamed grew frightened and strangled her. One man, in a good position, killed a woman who discovered that he had once been in prison for fraud and he was afraid that she would tell his employers.

It looks then as though the most plausible motives for murder that the detective-story writer can use are money, fear and revenge. Murder is a horrible thing and the murderer takes a great risk. It is hard to make your reader believe that he will take it because the girl he loves has given her affection to somebody else or because a colleague in a bank has been promoted over his head. The stakes he plays for must be high. The author's business is to persuade you that they are worth playing for.

III

At least equal in importance with the murderer is the detective. Every assiduous reader of crime stories can trip off a list of eminent sleuths, but the most famous is certainly Sherlock Holmes. For an anthology of short stories that I was preparing several years ago I re-read the collected stories of Conan Doyle. I was surprised to find how poor they were. The introduction is effective, the scene well set, but the anecdote is thin and you finish the tale with a sense of dissatisfaction. Great cry and little wool. I thought it necessary, however, to have one of these stories in an anthology that purported to be representative, but I had difficulty in finding even one that I thought the intelligent reader would be content to read. The fact remains that Sherlock Holmes caught and has held the public fancy. His name is a household word in every country in the civilised world. People know it who have never heard of Sir Willoughby Patterne, Monsieur Bergeret or Madame Verdurin. He was drawn in broad and telling lines, a melodramatic figure, with marked idiosyncrasies which Conan Doyle hammered into the minds of his readers with the same pertinacity as the great advertisers use to proclaim the merits of their soap, beer or cigarettes, and the results were as remunerative. You know no more of Sherlock Holmes after you have read fifty stories than you did after reading one, but the constant reiteration has broken down your resistance; and this lay figure, decked out with theatrical properties, has acquired the same sort of life in your imagination as is held by Vautrin or Mr. Micawber. No detective stories have had the popularity of Conan Doyle's, and because of the invention of Sherlock Holmes I think it may be admitted that none has so well deserved it.

Detectives are of three kinds. There is the police officer, the 'private eye', known also, I believe, as a shamus, and the amateur. The amateur has for long been very popular and the writers of this class of fiction have exerted their invention to devise a character that they could use again and again. The police officer is generally a conventional figure with little individuality; at best he is astute, painstaking and logical; but for the most part he is unimaginative and obtuse. Then of course he serves as a convenient foil to the amateur's brilliance. The amateur may be endowed with a number of distinctive features which give him some semblance of a human being. By discovering things that had escaped the inspector from Scotland Yard he can prove that the amateur is more intelligent and more competent than the professional, and this is naturally gratifying to the readers of a country in which the expert is always regarded with suspicion. The conflict between the two has a dramatic quality and, law-abiding as we may be, it does not displease us to see authority in the end made ridiculous. The most important of the traits which the writer takes care to attribute to his amateur detective is humour; and this not, as you might suppose, because by making your reader laugh you induce in him an emotional instability which will make him react more violently to your thrills; but for a much more important reason. It is very necessary that your amateur detective should by his wit or some absurd mannerism of speech arouse laughter, for if you can laugh at or with a character you cannot but have a certain sympathy with him; and to enlist your sympathy is here essential to the writer. For he has to use every means he can think of to conceal from you the patent fact that the amateur detective is a dirty dog.

He makes some show of working disinterestedly in the cause of justice, or if that is too much even for the readers of detective stories to swallow, that he is possessed by a passion for the chase; but the truth is that he is a busybody and a nosey-parker who from sheer love of interfering in what does not concern him engages in work which any decent person would leave to the officers of the law whose duty it is to do it. It is only by endowing him with engaging manners, an agreeable physique and lovable eccentricities that he can be made palatable to the reader. Above all he must have a line of amusing chatter. Unfortunately few of the writers of detective stories count a very delicate sense of humour among their accomplishments. Too many of them suppose that a joke can be repeated a hundred times and still amuse. Is it enough to make a character use English which is a literal, and often inaccurate, translation from the French to cause laughter? Is it enough to make him constantly quote or misquote hackneyed lines of verse or express himself in language of extravagant pomposity? Is it enough to use a Yorkshire dialect or reproduce an Irish brogue to make you split your sides? If it were, humorists would be two a penny, and neither Mr. P. G. Wodehouse nor Mr. S. J. Perelman would earn a living. I am still waiting for the story in which the amateur detective is shown as the despicable creature he really is and in the end gets his deserts.

I look upon the introduction of humour in a detective story as mistaken, but I see the reason for it and with a sigh accept it; on the other hand I have no patience with love interest. It may be that love makes the world go round, but not the world of detective stories; it makes it go very much askew. I do not care if it is the gentleman-like sleuth, the chief inspector or the wrongly accused hero who wins the girl in the end. In a detective story I want detection. The line is indicated – murder, inquiry, suspicion, discovery and punishment; and the philandering of young women, however charming, with young gentlemen, however lantern-jawed, is a tiresome diversion from the theme. Love of course is one of the springs of human action, and when it gives rise to jealousy, fear or wounded vanity may well serve the author's purpose, but it narrows the field of investigation; for presumably not more than two or three of the persons in your story are affected by its power; and when it is indeed the motive for murder this becomes a *crime passionnel* and the murderer ceases to be an object of unmitigated horror. But to introduce a pretty little love story in the unravelling of a mystery is an error of taste for which there is no excuse. Marriage bells have no place in a detective story.

I think another error that these writers often commit is to make the method of murder too far-fetched. Considering how vast is the output of these stories it is natural enough that they should seek to tempt the reader's jaded appetite by murders of an extraordinary character. I remember reading one in which several murders were perpetrated by means of poisonous fish introduced into a swimming pool. To my mind such ingenuities are mistaken. The probable, as we know, is relative, and only the fact that we accept it as such is the test of it.

In detective fiction we will accept a great deal; we will accept it that the murderer should leave on the scene of the crime a cigarette-end of an unusual make, muddy his shoes with a particular mould or scatter his finger-prints on my lady's chamber. We may all have our roof burnt over our heads and perish in the flames, be run over by an enemy's car, or pushed over a precipice; but we cannot believe that we shall ever be torn to pieces by a crocodile cunningly introduced into our sitting-room at the Dorchester or that when we are visiting the Louvre a villain by some fiendish machination will cause the Venus of Milo to fall and crush us as flat as a Dover sole. I think the classical methods still remain the best; the knife, the fire-arm, poison retain the advantages of probability. We may all fall victim to them or have occasion to use them.

The best writers of detective stories are those who give you the facts and the inferences to be drawn from them in readable English, but without any graces of style. Fine writing is here out of place. We do not want a purple passage to distract us when we hanker to know the meaning of that bruise on the butler's chin, nor do we want a description of scenery when the only thing that matters to us is to decide exactly how long it takes us to walk from the boat-house above the mill-race to the gamekeeper's cottage on the other side of the coppice. Nothing to us is the primrose by the river's brim. And in passing I may remark that I find it tedious to be asked by the aid of a map or a plan to make myself acquainted with the topography of the district or the lay-out of a house. Nor do we want erudition. The display of this has to my mind caused a sad falling off in one of the most ingenious and inventive of our contemporary masters of the detective story. She is a woman, I am told, of academic distinction and she has a remarkable knowledge of matters about which most of us are ignorant; but she would do better to keep it to herself. Of course it is galling to the writers of these clever books, which are read by everybody, high-brows, middle-brows and low-brows, that they should bring them so little credit. Are they invited to luncheon parties in Chelsea, or in Bloomsbury, or even in Mayfair? When publishers give their literary soirées do excited guests point them out to one another? Not more than a few of them are even known by name. The rest are enveloped in a vast anonymity of indifference.

It is natural that they should resent the patronising attitude which the very people who voraciously read their books adopt towards them, and should not be averse, when they have the chance, from drawing your attention to the fact that they are more refined and more cultivated than you appear to think. It is only human that they should wish to show the supercilious that they can be as learned as any Fellow of the Royal Society of Literature and as lyrical as any member of the Council of the Authors' Society. But it is a mistake. Let them be as strong as their own inspectors. It is very well that they should have wide information on all sorts of subjects, indeed they need it, but let them remark that the well-dressed man is he whose clothes you never notice; the culture of the detective-story writer should never distract attention from his proper business, which is to elucidate the mystery of a murder.

But let them have patience. It may well be that when the historians of literature come to discourse upon the fiction produced by the English-speaking peoples during the first half of this century they will pass somewhat lightly over the compositions of the 'serious' novelists and turn their attention to the immense and varied achievement of the detective writers. They will have to account first for the enormous popularity of this particular variety of fiction. They will be mistaken if they ascribe it to the increase of literacy which has created a huge body of avid but uneducated readers, for the 'whodunit', they will have to admit, was read also by men of learning and women of taste. My explanation is simple. The detective writers have a story to tell and they tell it briefly. They must capture and hold the reader's attention and so must get into their story with dispatch. They must arouse curiosity, excite suspense and by the invention of incident maintain the reader's interest. They must enlist his sympathy for the right characters, and the ingenuity with which they do this is not the least of their accomplishments. Finally they must work up to a satisfactory climax. They must in short follow the natural rules of story telling that have been followed ever since some nimblewitted fellow told the story of Joseph in the tents of Israel.

Now, the 'serious' novelists of today have often little or no story to tell; indeed they have allowed themselves to be persuaded that to tell a story is a negligible element in the art they practise. Thus they throw away their strongest appeal to our common human nature, for the desire to listen to stories is surely as old as the human race; and they have only themselves to blame if the writers of detective stories have stolen their readers from them. Moreover, they are often intolerably long-winded. They too seldom understand that a theme will only allow of a certain development and so will take four hundred pages to tell you what could be told in a hundred. They are encouraged to do this by the contemporary fashion for psychological analysis. To my mind the abuse of this is as harmful to the 'serious' fiction of today as was the abuse of the description of scenery in the novels of the nineteenth century. We have learnt now that descriptions of scenery should be short and should be used with the one and only purpose of getting on with the story. So should psychological analysis. In short, the detective writers are read because of their merits notwithstanding their often obvious defects: the 'serious' novelists remain in comparison little read because of their defects notwithstanding their often conspicuous merits.

IV

Hitherto I have dealt with the simple story of detection founded on the principles laid down by Poe in *The Murders in the Rue Morgue*. During the last half-century such stories have been written by the thousand and their authors have used every possible expedient to give them a specious novelty. I have already referred to murder by unusual means. Authors have been quick to make use of every new scientific and medical discovery. They have stabbed their victims with sharp icicles, electrocuted them by telephone, injected air bubbles into their blood vessels, infected their shaving brushes with anthrax bacilli, killed them by making them lick poisoned stamps, shot them with guns concealed in cameras and polished them off by invisible death rays. These extravagant methods are too improbable to carry conviction.

Sometimes of course authors have shown remarkable ingenuity. One of their cleverest inventions has been what is known as the locked room puzzle: a dead man, obviously murdered, is found in a room locked from the inside so that the murderer could apparently neither have got in or out. Poe used the idea in *The Murders in the Rue Morgue*. It is surprising that the critics have never noticed that his explanation of the mystery is demonstrably false. When, as the reader will remember, the neighbours, roused by terrific shrieks, broke into the house inhabited by the two women, mother and daughter, whom they found murdered, the daughter was found in a room locked from the inside with the windows securely fastened also from within. Monsieur Dupin proves that the giant ape which had killed them had got in by an open window and this had closed by its own weight after the beast's escape. Any policeman would have informed him that two Frenchwomen, one old and the other middle-aged, would *never* have left a window open to let in the noxious airs of night. However the ape got into the house it was not through an open window. The device has since then been most ably used by Carter Dickson, but his success has produced so many imitators that it has by now lost its savour.

Every background has been utilised – the country house party in Sussex, Long Island or Florida, the quiet village in which nothing has happened since the Battle of Waterloo, the castle in the Hebrides isolated by a storm. So have clues – finger-prints, foot-prints, cigarette-ends, perfume, powder. So have unbreakable alibis which the detective breaks, the dog that does not bark, thus pointing to the fact that it was familiar with the murderer (this was first used, I think, by Conan Doyle), the code letter which the detective deciphers, the identical twins and secret passages. Readers no longer have patience with the girl who wanders about deserted corridors for no adequate reason and gets knocked on the head by a hooded, masked figure; nor with the girl who insists on accompanying the detective on a dangerous errand and by so doing makes a mess of his plans. All these settings, all these clues, all these puzzles have been worked to death. Of this, of course, the authors have grown well aware and they have sought to give interest to stories that have been told a hundred times already by inventions more and more extravagant. All in vain. Every method of murder, every finesse of detection, every guile to throw the reader off the scent, every scene of action in every class of life, has been used again and again. The story of pure deduction has run to seed.

It has been replaced in the public favour by the 'hard-boiled' story. This is said to have been invented by Dashiell Hammett, but Erle Stanley Gardner claims that the first to write it was a certain John Daly. In any case it was Hammett's *The Maltese Falcon* that created the vogue. The hard-boiled story purports to be realistic. Duchesses, cabinet ministers, wealthy industrialists seldom get murdered. Murders seldom take place in great country houses, on golf links or at race meetings. They are seldom committed by elderly maiden ladies or retired diplomatists. Raymond Chandler, the most brilliant author now writing this kind of story, in his sensible and amusing essay, *The Simple Art of Murder*, specifies the constituents of the genre. 'The realist in murder,' he says, 'writes of a world in which gangsters can rule nations and almost rule cities, in which hotels and apartment houses and celebrated restaurants are owned by men who made their money out of brothels, in which a screen star can be the fingerman for a mob, and a nice man down the hall is a boss of the numbers racket; a world where a judge with a cellar full of bootleg liquor can send a man to jail for having a pint in his pocket, where the mayor of your town may have condoned murder as an instrument of money-making, where no man can walk down a dark alley in safety because law and order are things we talk about but refrain from practising, a world where you may witness a hold-up in broad daylight and see who did it, but you will quickly fade back into the crowd rather than tell anyone, because the hold-up man may have friends with long guns or the police may not like your testimony, and in any case the shyster for the defence will be allowed to abuse and vilify you in open court, before a jury of selected morons, without any but the most perfunctory interference from a political judge.'

All this is very well put and it is evident that such a state of society offers the realistic author suitable matter for a story of crime. The reader is willing to believe that the incidents related actually happened; indeed, he has only to read the newspapers to know that such things are happening far from seldom.

'Dashiell Hammett,' as Raymond Chandler says, 'gave

murder back to the kind of people that commit it for reasons, not just to provide a corpse, and with the means at hand, not with hand-wrought duelling pistols, curare and tropical fish. He put these people down on paper as they are, and he made them talk and think in the language they customarily used for their purposes.' This is high praise and it is justified. Hammett had been for eight years a Pinkerton detective and he knew the world of which he wrote. It enabled him to give a plausibility to his stories which has been equalled only by Raymond Chandler himself.

In the novels of this school actual detection takes a relatively minor place. No great secret is made of the murderer's identity and the interest of the story depends on the detective's efforts to fasten the guilt on him and the dangers he incurs while doing so. A consequence of this is that the writers have discarded the tiresome use of clues. In fact, in *The Maltese Falcon*, Sam Spade, the detective, pins the murder of Archer on Brigid O'Shaughnessy by pointing out to her that she is the only person who *could* have committed it, whereupon she loses her presence of mind and admits it. If she hadn't done this, but had coolly answered 'Prove it', he would have been nonplussed; and in any case had she got Perry Mason, Erle Stanley Gardner's astute lawyer, to defend her, no jury would have convicted her on the flimsy evidence which was all that Spade had to produce.

The authors who specialise in the hard-boiled story have been at pains to give their detectives character and personality, but have mercifully refrained from giving them the extravagant oddities with which in imitation of Conan Doyle many of the writers of 'pure' detective stories have thought fit to endow their sleuths.

Dashiell Hammett is an inventive and original writer. Unlike the authors who use the same detective over and over again, he has created a different one for every story. The detective in *The Dane Curse* appears to be a fat, middle-aged man who depends on his wits and his nerve rather than upon his brawn; Nick Charles in *The Thin Man* has married a wife with money and retired from the business, which he resumes only on pressure; he is a pleasant fellow, with a sense of humour; Ned Beaumont in *The Glass Key*, a professional gambler and only a detective by accident, is a curious, intriguing character whom any novelist would have been proud to conceive; Sam Spade, in *The Maltese Falcon*, is the best of them all and the most convincing. He is an unscrupulous rogue and a heartless crook. He is himself so nearly a criminal that there is little to choose between him and the criminals he is dealing with. He is a nasty bit of goods, but he is admirably depicted.

Sherlock Holmes was a private detective, but the authors who came after Conan Doyle seem to have preferred to solve their mysteries by means of a police inspector or a brilliant amateur. Dashiell Hammett, having been himself a private detective, very naturally used private detectives when he came to write stories, and his successors in the hard-boiled school have very wisely followed his good example. The 'private eye' is at once a romantic and a sinister figure. Like the amateur he can be cleverer than members of the force and he can do things, mostly shady, which they are by law forbidden to do. He has the further advantage that, since the District Attorney and the police regard his unorthodox methods with suspicion, he has to fight them as well as the criminal. It adds tension and dramatic conflict to the story. Finally he has the advantage over the amateur detective that as it is his business to deal with crime he cannot be regarded as a busybody who pokes his nose into what is no concern of his. But why he has adopted this unsavoury profession we are not told. It does not appear to be a lucrative one, for he is always short of money, and his office is small and poorly furnished. We are told little about his antecedents. He seems to have neither father, mother, uncles, aunts, brothers or sisters.

On the other hand he is fortunate in having a secretary who is blonde, beautiful and loving. He treats her with kindly affection and now and again rewards her devotion with a kiss, but so far as I can remember is never so far carried away as to make her a proposal of marriage. Though (with the exception of Chandler's Philip Marlow) we are not told where he comes from nor how he acquired the knowledge to pursue his avocation, we are told a good deal about his person and his habits. He is irresistible to women. He is tall and strong and tough, and can knock a man out as easily as we can swat a fly. He can take any amount of punishment without permanent injury, for he has more courage than prudence, and will put himself, often unarmed, in the power of dangerous criminals who beat him up so brutally that you are astonished to find him up and about in a day or so apparently none the worse for it, and he will take risks so hazardous that you hold your breath. The suspense, indeed, would be unbearable if you did not know that the gangsters, crooks and blackmailers who have him at their mercy dare not riddle him with bullets or your novel would come to an untimely end. He has remarkable power of absorbing hard liquor. In the drawer of his desk there is always a bottle of rye or bourbon which he gets out whenever he has a caller and whenever he has nothing else to do. He keeps a flask in his hip-pocket and a pint in the glove-compartment of his car. The first thing he does when he arrives at an hotel is to send the bell-boy for a bottle. His staple diet, like that of most Americans, has a certain monotony about it and consists for the most part of bacon and eggs or steak and 'French fried'. The only 'private eye' that I can remember who cares what he eats is Nero Wolf, but he is a mid-European and his un-American addiction to succulent victuals, like his passion for orchids, must be ascribed to his foreign birth.

The social historian of the future may notice with surprise what is plainly a difference in American habits between the time when Dashiell Hammett wrote his stories and the time when Raymond Chandler wrote his. After an exhausting day passed in heavy drinking and hair-breadth escapes from violent death Ned Beaumont changes his collar and washes his hands and face, but Raymond Chandler's Marlow, unless my memory deceives me, has a shower and puts on a clean shirt. It is evident that the habit of cleanliness had in the interval gained an increasing hold on the American male. Marlow, unlike Sam Spade, is an honest man. He wants to make money, but will only earn it by lawful means, and he will not touch divorce. Marlow is himself the narrator of the too few stories Raymond Chandler has written. Usually the narrator and protagonist of a novel remains a shadowy character, as for instance is David Copperfield, but Raymond Chandler has succeeded in making Marlow a vivid human being. He is a hard, fierce, fearless man and a very likeable fellow.

To my mind the two best novelists of the hard-boiled school are Dashiell Hammett and Raymond Chandler. Raymond Chandler is the more accomplished. Sometimes Hammett's story is so complicated that you are not a trifle confused: Raymond Chandler maintains an unswerving line. His pace is swifter. He deals with a more varied assortment of persons. He has a greater sense of probability and his motivation is more plausible. Both write a nervous, colloquial English racy of the American soil. Raymond Chandler's dialogue seems to me better than Hammett's. He has an admirable aptitude for that typical product of the quick American mind, the wisecrack, and his sardonic humour has an engaging spontaneity.

The hard-boiled novel, as I have said, lays little stress on the detection of crime. It is concerned with the people, crooks, gamblers, thieves, blackmailers, corrupt policemen, dishonest politicians, who commit crimes. Incidents occur, but incidents derive their interest from the individuals who are concerned in them. If they are merely lay-figures you do not care what they do or what happens to them. The result of this is that the writers of this school have had to pay more attention to characterisation than the old writers of the story of deduction found necessary. They have had to make their people not only credible, but convincing. Most of the older detectives were creatures of farce and the extravagant oddities their authors gave them succeeded only in making them grotesque. Such persons never existed but in their begetters' wrong-headedness. The other actors in their stories were stock characters without individuality. Dashiell Hammett and Raymond Chandler have created characters that we can believe in. They are only a little more heightened, a little more vivid, than people we have all come across.

Having been at one time a novelist myself I have been interested in the way both these authors describe the appearance of the various persons they deal with. It is always difficult to give the reader an exact impression of what someone looks like and novelists have tried various methods to achieve it. Hammett and Raymond Chandler specify the appearance of their characters and the clothes they wear, though briefly, as exactly as do the police when they send to the papers a description of a wanted man. Raymond Chandler has effectively pursued the method further. When Marlow, his detective, enters a room or an office we are told concisely, but in detail, precisely what furniture is in it, what pictures hang on the walls and what rugs lie on the floor. We are impressed by the detective's power of observation. It is done as neatly as a playwright (if he is not as verbose as Bernard Shaw) describes for his director the scene and the furnishings of each act of his play. The device cleverly gives the perspicacious reader an indication of the sort of person and the circumstances the detective is likely to encounter. When you know a man's surroundings you already know something about the man.

But I think the enormous success these two writers

have had, not only financial, for their books have sold by the million, but critical, has killed the genre. Dozens of imitators have sprung up. Like all imitators they have thought by exaggeration to improve upon their models. They have been more slangy, so slangy that you need a glossary to know what they are talking about; their criminals have been more brutal, more violent, more sadistic; their female characters have been more blonde and more man-crazy; their detectives have been more unscrupulous and more alcoholic; and their policemen have been more inept and more corrupt. In fact they have been so outrageous that they have become preposterous. In their frantic search for sensationalism they have numbed their readers and instead of horrifying them have caused them to laugh with derision. There is only one of the many merits of the two authors I have been discussing that they do not seem to have thought worth copying. They have made no attempt to write good English.

I do not see who can succeed Raymond Chandler. I believe the detective story, both the story of pure deduction and the hard-boiled story, is dead. But that will not prevent a multitude of authors from continuing to write such stories, nor will it prevent me from continuing to read them.

After Reading Burke

I

I am the happy possessor of the complete works of Hazlitt and from time to time I take a volume from my shelves and read an essay here, an essay there, as my inclination prompts. I am seldom disappointed. Like every writer he is not always at his best, which is very good indeed, but even at his worst he is readable. He is amusing, bitter, keen-witted, violent, sympathetic, unjust, generous; he scarcely ever wrote a page in which he does not give you himself, with his faults and his virtues; and that in the end is all an author has to give. The assiduous reader of Hazlitt cannot fail to notice how often the name of Edmund Burke appears in his pages. It never ceases to give me a little thrill when I find him referred to as 'the late Mr. Burke'; the hundred and fifty years that have passed since his death seem then to be no great matter and I feel that he was, if not a contemporary of my own, someone whom if I had been fortunate I might have known in my youth as, for example, I might have known George Meredith or Swinburne. Hazlitt was of opinion that Burke was the first prose writer of his time and in one of his essays states that at one period of his life his three favourite writers were Burke, Junius and Rousseau. 'I was never weary,' he says, 'of admiring and wondering at the felicities of the style, the turns of expression, the refinements of thought and sentiment: I laid the book down to find out the secret of so much strength and beauty, and took it up again in despair, to read on and admire.' In passage after passage Hazlitt praises Burke's style and it is evident that his own owes a good deal to his study of it. He describes him with the exception of Jeremy Taylor, the most poet of prose writers. 'It has always appeared to me,' he says, 'that the most perfect prose-style, the most powerful, the most dazzling, the most daring, that which went the nearest to the verge of poetry and yet never fell over, was Burke's. It has the solidity and the sparkling effect of the diamond ... Burke's style is airy, flighty, adventurous, but it never loses sight of the subject; nay, is always in contact with, and derives its increased and varying impulse from it.' And again: 'His style has all the familiarity of conversation, and all the research of the most elaborate conversation. He says what he wants to say, by any means, nearer or more remote within his reach. He makes use of the most common or scientific terms, of the longest or shortest sentences, of the plainest and most downright, or of the most figurative modes of speech ... He everywhere gives the image he wishes to give, in its true and appropriate colouring; and it is the very crowd and variety of these images that have given his language its peculiar tone of animation and even of passion. It is his impatience to transfer his conceptions entire, living, in all their rapidity, strength and glancing variety – to the minds of others, that constantly pushes him to the verge of extravagance, and yet supports him there in dignified security.'

This, and other passages too numerous or too long to cite, so much impressed me that I thought I should like to see for myself what justification there was for praise so unqualified. I had not read Burke since I was very young; I read then *On Conciliation with the Colonies* and *On the Affairs with America*; perhaps owing to my youth I did not find the matter very interesting, but I was deeply affected by the manner and I retained the recollection, vivid though vague, of a splendid magniloquence. I have now read these speeches once more, and the more important writings of Burke besides, and in the following pages I wish to submit to the reader the reflections that have occurred to me. I hasten, however, to tell him that I do not propose to deal with Burke's thought; for that it would be necessary to have a much greater knowledge of the eighteenth century than I can claim and an interest in, and a familiarity with, the principles of politics which I must admit (and it may be I should admit with shame) I am far from possessing. I desire to treat only of the manner in which Burke wrote without paying any more attention than can be helped to the matter of which he wrote. It is evident that the two can never be entirely separated, for style must be conditioned by the subject of discourse; a grave, balanced and deliberate manner befits an important theme, but has a grotesque effect when it is applied to a trivial one: contrariwise a gay, sparkling way of writing is ill-suited to those great topics of which Dr. Johnson remarked that you could no longer say anything new about them that was true or anything true about them that was new. But if writers must continue to speak of them they err when they try to excite our interest by jumping through verbal hoops and turning paradoxical somersaults. One of the difficulties that the novelist has to cope with is that his style must change with his matter and if he tries to keep it uniform he will find it hard to avoid an impression of artificiality; for he must be colloquial when he reports dialogue, rapid when he narrates action, and restrained or impassioned (according to his idiosyncrasy) when he describes emotion. But perhaps it is enough if the novelist contents himself with avoiding the grosser errors of grammar, for no one can have considered this matter without being struck by the significant and surprising fact that the four greatest novelists the world has seen, Tolstoi, Balzac, Dostoevsky and Dickens, wrote their respective languages very carelessly; and Dickens, as we know, did not even take the trouble to write tolerable grammar. It is for the historian, the divine and the essayist to acquire and maintain a settled style and it is no accident that in this country the most splendid monuments of the English language have been produced by such essayists as Sir Thomas Browne, Dryden, Addison and Johnson (for *Rasselas*, though purposing to be a work of fiction, is in effect an essay on the vanity of human wishes), by such divines as Jeremy Taylor and William Law, and by such historians as Gibbon. Among these Edmund Burke holds an eminent place.

Hazlitt says that he had tried half a dozen times to describe Burke's style without succeeding, and it may seem presumptuous in me to attempt something that Hazlitt failed to do; but, in fact, in various of his essays he has given so good a description of it that there is really nothing left to add. He takes note of its severe extravagance; its literal boldness; its matter-of-fact hyperbole; its running away with a subject, and from it at the same time; and then he adds, 'but there is no making it out, for there is no example of the same thing anywhere else. We have no common measure to refer to; and his qualities contradict even themselves.' My object is not to describe Burke's style, but to examine its texture and to discover, if I can, the methods he employed by means of words to produce his effects. Hazlitt has set forth the rich succulence of the dish; my aim is to ferret out the ingredients that give it savour. I am concerned to find out how he constructed his sentences and how he ordered his paragraphs, what use he made of abstract and concrete words, of image and metaphor, and of what rhetorical devices he availed himself to serve his turn; and if this seems a dull subject, after all no one is under an obligation to read the following pages. To me, a writer, it is an interesting one. But I am confronted with two difficulties: the first is that I am none too confident of my capacity to deal with this somewhat ambitious task; the second is that I can only hope to achieve a measure of success by giving quotations, and these I believe only the most conscientious readers can resist the temptation to skip. Yet it is only by example that I can indicate practice. English is a difficult language to write, and few authors have written it consistently with accuracy and distinction. The best way of learning to do this is to study the great masters of the past. Much of what Burke wrote has no longer, except perhaps to the politician, a pressing interest; indeed, I believe that almost all that he has to say of value to the average reader now could be put into one volume of elegant extracts; and for my part I must confess that I could never have brought myself to read his voluminous works with such care if I had not hoped to gain something from them that would enable me to write more nearly as I wish to. The manner of writing changes with the fleeting generations and it would be absurd to try to write now like one of the great stylists of the eighteenth century, but I see no reason to suppose that they have not something to teach us that may be to our purpose. The language of literature maintains its vitality by absorbing the current speech of the people; this gives it colour, vividness and actuality; but if it is to avoid shapelessness and incoherence it must be founded on, and determined by, the standards of the period when English prose attained the highest degree of perfection of which it seems capable.

I think there are few writers who write well by nature. Burke was a man of prodigious industry and it is certain that he took pains not only over the matter of his discourse, but over the manner. 'With respect to his facility of composition,' says Hazlitt, 'there are contrary accounts. It has been stated by some that he wrote out a plain sketch first, like a sort of dead colouring, and added the ornaments and tropes afterwards. I have been assured by a person who had the best means of knowing, that the *Letter to a Noble Lord* (the most rapid, impetuous, glancing and sportive of all his works) was printed off, and the proof sent to him: and that it was returned to the printing-office with so many alterations and passages inter-lined, that the compositors refused to correct it as it was – took the whole matter in pieces, and re-set the copy. This looks like elaboration and afterthought.' And we learn from Dodsley that more than a dozen revises of the *Reflections on the French Revolution* were taken off and destroyed before the author could satisfy himself. A glance at the *Origin of Our Ideas of the Sublime and Beautiful* is enough to show that Burke's style was the result of labour. Though this work, praised by Johnson, turned to account by Lessing and esteemed by Kant, cannot now be read with great profit it may still afford entertainment. In arguing that perfection is not the cause of beauty, he asserts: 'Women are very sensible of this; for which reason they learn to lisp, to totter in their walk, to counterfeit weakness, and even sickness. In all this they are guided by nature. Beauty in distress is much the most affecting beauty. Blushing has little less power; and modesty in general, which is a tacit allowance of imperfection, is itself considered as an amiable quality, and certainly heightens every other that is so. I know it is in everybody's mouth, that we ought to love perfection. This is to me a sufficient proof that it is not the proper object of love.' Here is another quotation: 'When we have before us such objects as excite love and complacency, the body is affected so far as I could observe, much in the following manner: the head reclines something on one side, the eyelids are more closed than usual, and the eyes roll gently with an inclination to the object; the mouth is a little opened, and the breath drawn slowly, with now and then a long sigh; the whole body is composed, and the hands fall idly to the sides.' This book is supposed to have been first written when Burke was nineteen and it was published when he was twenty-six. I have given these quotations to show the style in which he wrote before he submitted to the influence which enabled him to become one of the masters of English prose. It is the general manner of the middle of the eighteenth century and I doubt whether anyone who read these passages would know who was the author. It is correct, easy and flowing; it shows that Burke had by nature a good ear. English is a language of harsh consonants, and skill is needed to avoid the juxtaposition of sounds that offend the hearing. Some authors are insensible to this and will use a word ending with a consonant, or even a pair of them, and put beside it a word beginning with the same one or the same pair (a fast stream); they will use alliteration (always dangerous in prose) and will write words that rhyme (thus producing an unpleasant jingle) without any feeling of discomfort. Of course the sense is the first thing, but the riches of the English language are such that it is seldom a sufficiently exact synonym cannot be found for the word that comes first to mind. It is seldom that an author is obliged to let something stand that grates upon his ear because only so can he say precisely what he wants to. One of the most valuable things that can be learnt from Burke is that, however unmanageable certain words may appear, it is possible by proper placing, the judicious admixture of long ones with short, by alternation of consonants and vowels and by alternation of accent, to secure euphony. Of course no one could write at all if he bore these considerations in his conscious mind; the ear does the work. In Burke's case I think it evident that the natural sensibility of the organ was infinitely developed by the exigencies of public speech: even when he wrote only to be read the sound of the spoken phrase was present to him. He was not a melodious writer as Jeremy Taylor was in the seventeenth century or Newman in the nineteenth; his prose has force, vitality and speed rather than beauty; but notwithstanding the intricate complication of many of his sentences they remain easy to say and good to hear. I have no doubt that at times Burke wrote a string of words that was neither and in the tumult of his passion broke the simple rules of euphony which I have indicated. An author has the right to be judged by his best.

I have read somewhere that Burke learnt to write by studying Spenser and it appears that many of his gorgeous sentences and poetical allusions can be traced to the poet. He himself said that: 'Whoever relishes and reads Spenser as he ought to be read, will have a strong hold of the English language.' I do not see what he can have acquired from that mellifluous but (to my mind) tedious bard other than that sense of splendid sound of which I have just been speaking. He was certainly never influenced by the excessive use of alliteration which (again to my mind) makes the *Faerie Queene* cloying and sometimes even absurd. It has been said, among others by Charles James Fox, who should have known, that Burke founded his style on Milton's. I cannot believe it. It is true that he often quoted him and it would be strange indeed if with his appreciation of fine language Burke had failed to be impressed by the magnificence of vocabulary and grandeur of phrase in *Paradise Lost*; but the *Letters on a Regicide Peace*, on which, such as it is, the evidence for the statement rests, were written in old age: it seems improbable that if Burke had really studied Milton's prose for the purpose of forming his own its influence should not have been apparent till he had one foot in the grave. Nor can I believe, as the *Dictionary of National Biography* asserts, that he founded it on Dryden's. I see in Burke's deliberate, ordered and resonant prose no trace of Dryden's charming grace and happy-go-lucky facility. There is all the difference that there is between a French garden of trim walks and ordered parterres and a Thames-side park with its coppices and its green meadows. For my part I think it more likely that the special character of Burke's settled manner must be ascribed to the robust and irresistible example of Dr. Johnson. I think it was from him that Burke learnt the value of a long intricate sentence, the potent force of polysyllabic words, the rhetorical effect of balance and the epigrammatic elegance of antithesis. He avoided Johnson's faults (small faults to those who like myself have a peculiar fondness for Johnson's style) by virtue of his affluent and impetuous fancy and his practice of public speaking.

II

We all know Buffon's dictum that *Le style c'est l'homme même*. If it is true, then by making yourself acquainted with the man it should be possible to come to a better understanding of his style. But is it true? I think Buffon thought men more of a piece than they really are. They are for the most part an amalgam of virtues and vices, of strengths and weaknesses so incompatible that it is only because they are manifest that you can believe it possible for them to co-exist in one and the same person. Burke was much discussed in his day, passionately praised by some, violently decried by others, and from the various reports that have come down to us, from Hazlitt's essays and the excellent *Life* of Sir Philip Magnus, it is possible, I think, to get a fairly accurate impression of the kind of man he was. But it is not a plausible one. It is with difficulty that you can persuade yourself to believe that merits so rare can go hand-in-hand with defects so deplorable. You are left utterly perplexed.

Edmund Burke was born in Ireland, in 1729, the son of an attorney, a profession then held in small respect: Johnson once remarked of someone who had quitted the company that 'he did not care to speak ill of any man behind his back, but he believed the gentleman was an *attorney*.' When just over twenty Burke went to London to study law and soon after his arrival formed a close friendship with a certain William Burke who, if a relation at all, was a very distant one. He soon abandoned the law for literature and for some years made his living as best he could by writing for the booksellers. He published a couple of books which appear to have attracted sufficient attention to secure him the acquaintance of Horace Walpole and the warm friendship of Dr. Johnson. He married in 1757 and the same year his younger brother Richard joined him in London. The three Burkes were devoted to one another; William and Richard lived with Edmund and his wife, and they shared a common purse. Richard was a noisy, exuberant, disreputable fellow without, as far as one can tell, any redeeming qualities; but William was able and pushing. He had made useful friends at Oxford and when in 1765 Lord Rockingham was called upon by the King to form a ministry he persuaded him to offer Edmund the post of his private secretary and got Lord Verney to give him one of the pocket boroughs at his disposal.

Burke immediately made his mark in the House of Commons. Dr. Johnson wrote to Bennet Langton that he had 'gained more reputation than perhaps any man at his first appearance ever gained before. He made two speeches in the House for repealing the Stamp Act, which were publicly commended by Mr. Pitt, and have filled the town with wonder.' The ministry fell in 1766 and two years later Burke bought a house called Gregories with an estate of six hundred acres at Beaconsfield. It is natural enough that he should have wished to do this. His reputation was great and he had a well-justified confidence in his ability. We may suppose that his lofty spirit, his boisterous exuberance, made it irksome to him to live meanly. He was a sociable creature and loved to entertain his friends. It was a pleasure to him to succour deserving (and often undeserving) talent and to relieve the necessities of the needy. His origins were modest and such were the manners of the time it may be that he was often twitted with them. He lived in the company of the great; he was used by his party and knew himself to be invaluable, but he could not be unaware that he was regarded with suspicion; he was with them, but not of them, and there hung about him the taint of the Irish adventurer. And that of course is exactly what he was; he happened to be also a man of high principle, brilliant gifts, social and intellectual, and wide knowledge. He may well have thought that the acquisition of Gregories, by giving him a stake in the country, would add to his prestige and, by enabling him to meet these lords and gentlemen on a more equal footing, increase the influence on them which till then he had owed only to his talents.

The estate cost twenty thousand pounds and twenty-five hundred a year to keep up. It seemed strange that a man who a few years before had been glad to accept from Dodsley, the bookseller, a hundred pounds a year to do hackwork could think of disbursing so large a sum and be prepared to burden himself with an expense so great. The Burkes, with Lord Verney to back them, were engaged in vast gambling transactions in East India Stock and they seem to have bought Gregories on the profits they had made; but then, unfortunately for them, the stock fell heavily, they were unable to meet their differences, and in the end Lord Verney was ruined and William Burke fled the country. Edmund, involved in financial difficulties which harassed him to the end of his life, was obliged to mortgage the property 'up to the hilt' and borrow money from his friends. The year he bought Gregories he borrowed a thousand pounds from David Garrick, and at some later date two thousand more from Sir Joshua Reynolds. During the seventeen years of his connection with Rockingham he received from him loans amounting to thirty thousand pounds. Now it is a common experience that when sums of money of any extent have passed from one person to another there arises a constraint between them that often results in coldness. In Burke's case, such was the esteem in which his friends held him, nothing of the sort happened. They revered his 'private virtues and transcendent worth', and it may be supposed that, like Dr. Brocklesby who made him a present of a thousand pounds, they gave him the money he so badly needed as proof of their devotion. When Rockingham died he left instructions that Burke's bonds should be destroyed. Reynolds did the same thing and left him a couple of thousand pounds besides.

Burke was a proud man, sensitive of his honour, and one asks oneself if he did not feel it a humiliation to apply to his friends for money. It seems never to have occurred to him that he could very well sell Gregories and by paying his debts extricate himself from a situation that was not only mortifying but damaging to his reputation. One can only suppose that he looked upon it as an asset of such consequence that it must be retained at whatever cost to his dignity. And of course it is only a surmise that he looked upon the situation as mortifying. Borrowing, as we know, is a habit easy to contract, hard to break, and the habitual borrower soon finds a way to satisfy his need and retain his self-respect.

Burke had the insouciance which is generally considered a characteristic of the Irish in money matters, and he had also their generous warm-heartedness.

However hard pressed, he continued to give financial aid to those who enlisted his sympathies. There was an Irish painter, James Barry by name, whom he mistakenly thought a genius and to whom he gave an income so that he might study in Italy. Crabbe, the poet, was destitute; the applications he had made to one distinguished person and another for help went unanswered and as a last resource he applied to Burke. Burke installed him at Gregories and never rested till he saw him comfortably settled for life. These are only two instances of his constant benefactions. Few people came in contact with him without growing conscious of his greatness. It is remarkable how often one comes across references to the veneration with which he was regarded; so frequent are they that I have asked myself whether the word had then a slightly different connotation from what it has now. I have respect and admiration for the statesmen, generals and admirals who conducted affairs during the last war. I esteem the great gifts of the poets and novelists with whom it has been my good fortune to be acquainted, but it has never occurred to me, nor, I imagine, to anybody else, to look upon them with veneration. Perhaps we no longer possess the faculty of doing so. Burke had charm, and until worry and disappointment soured him a genial temper. He was a great talker and, as we know, Dr. Johnson valued him for the 'affluence of his conversation'. I have asked myself how this would please us at the present day. It is hard to avoid the impression that we should find it a trifle heavy, for it appears to have been devastatingly informative, and we are inclined to be impatient of being told what we can read for ourselves, if not in a book, in the newspapers. We are no better listeners than was Burke himself (Johnson complained that: 'So desirous is he to talk that if one is speaking at one end of the table, he'll speak to somebody at the other end'), and we are restless of a talker who monopolises the conversation. And Burke had neither wit nor humour. It is possible that we should think him something of a bore, and I am afraid that, notwithstanding the commanding air and fine presence that impressed Fanny Burney, we should prefer to his eloquence the playful flippancy of Miss Austen's Henry Tilney.

After the crash of East India Stock, Richard Burke, who by Edmund's influence had some years before been appointed Receiver-General of His Majesty's revenues in the West India island of Granada, returned to his post. He bought for next-door to nothing from the Red Caribbees, descendants of the indigenous inhabitants of the neighbouring island of St. Vincent, a great tract of land which was estimated to be worth a hundred thousand pounds. The transaction was so disreputable that the Council of St. Vincent refused to admit its legality. The Burkes were by this time in desperate straits and Edmund made every effort to have his brother's claim substantiated. He offered Fox, himself badly in need of money, a share of the swag if he could induce Lord North, then in office, to rule that the purchase was valid. Fox tried, and Lord North was apparently prepared to oblige, but he bungled the matter and Richard, defeated, returned to England. He was then charged with misappropriating ten thousand pounds of His Majesty's revenues, tried and found guilty. He appealed. Burke used his influence to have the appeal indefinitely postponed. One would think that had he been convinced of his brother's innocence he would have been glad to see it proved. William Burke, on leaving England to escape being arrested for debt, went to India, and there, again by Edmund's interest, was appointed Paymaster of the King's Troops. He engaged in a variety of shady enterprises, from one of which he expected to net a hundred and fifty thousand pounds and which Sir Philip Magnus describes as flagrantly dishonest. When, utterly discredited, he was obliged to return to England he was in danger of being arrested for embezzlement. A pretty pair!

Much of this dirty business was not known till Sir Philip examined the papers at Wentworth Woodhouse, but enough leaked out gravely to discredit Edmund. Dr. Johnson was a shrewd judge of character and he retained his affection for him till his death. He valued Burke's intelligence, his knowledge, his amiability and his benevolence, but there are passages in Boswell which suggest that even he doubted his honesty. It is true that during the eighteenth century it was an understood thing that they who served the State had the right to live on it. But Burke was a moralist and a reformer. He prided himself on his high principles, and yet could use his power to get men appointed to lucrative offices for which they were notoriously unfitted. He prided himself on his veracity, and yet could untruthfully make a public declaration that he had never had dealings in East India Stock. He consistently fought injustice and corruption, and yet strained every nerve to further the corrupt and unjust chicaneries of William and Richard. Burke was a great orator; it was difficult to reconcile his admirable precepts with his reprehensible practice and it is no wonder that people said he was a humbug and a hypocrite. I don't think he was. He had to an extreme degree the failing, common to most men, and one to which politicians are not immune, of believing what it was to his interest to believe. He would not look at what he did not want to see. I don't know what name to give to this failing, but neither hypocrisy nor humbug is the right one. When Burke's affections were engaged his judgment was vitiated. It was the misfortune of his life that his most engaging trait, his power of affection, should have had such unhappy consequences. William and Richard were a pair of crooks, and not even clever crooks, for not one of their nefarious schemes succeeded; yet Edmund could write: 'Looking back to the course of my life I remember no one considerable merit in the whole course of it which I did not, mediately or immediately, derive from William Burke.' And of Richard he wrote that his integrity was such that no temptation could corrupt it. He loved them both to the end and, incredible as it may seem, respected them. In his eyes they could do no wrong and so, no matter how damning was the evidence against them, he disbelieved it.

'If a man were to go by chance at the same time with Burke under a shed, to shun a shower,' said Dr. Johnson, 'he would say – "this is an extraordinary man".' Burke was extraordinary in more ways than Johnson knew. It is not often that you come across a man the features of whose personality are so incompatible as was the case with Burke. He was upright and abject, straightforward and shifty, disinterested and corrupt. How is one to reconcile characteristics so discordant? I don't know. But let us not be censorious. Did not Becky Sharp say that it was easy to be good on five thousand a year?

If Burke had been born a gentleman with a fine estate and an ample income his conduct would doubtless have been as irreproachable as he was invariably convinced it was. About that, the propriety of his conduct, he never had a doubt and he looked upon the obloquy (his own word) with which he was pursued as a shameful injustice. Machiavelli has told us that when he retired to his study to write he discarded his country clothes and donned the damask robe in which as Secretary of the Republic he was wont to appear before the Signoria. So, in spirit, did Burke. In his study he was no longer the reckless punter, the shameless sponge, the unscrupulous place-hunter (not for himself, but for others), the dishonest advocate who attacked measures introduced to correct scandalous abuses because his pocket would be affected by their passage. In his study he was the high-minded man whom his friends loved and honoured for his nobility of spirit, his greatness and his magnanimity. In his study he was the honest man he was assured he was. Then, but only then, you can say of Burke: *Le style c'est l'homme même.*

III

His style, it must be obvious, is solidly based on balance. Hazlitt stated that it was Dryden who first used balance in the formation of his sentences. That seems an odd thing to say since one would have thought that balance came naturally to anyone who added two sentences together by a copulative: there is balance of a sort when you say: 'He went out for a walk and came home wet through'. Dr. Johnson on the other hand, speaking of Dryden's prose, said: 'The clauses are never balanced, nor the periods modelled: every word seems to drop by chance, though it falls in its proper place.' Thus do authorities disagree. Burke was much addicted to what for want of a better word I will call the triad; by this I mean the juxtaposition of three nouns, three adjectives, three clauses to reinforce a point. Here are some examples: 'Never was cause supported with more constancy, more activity, more spirit.' – 'Shall there be no reserve power in the Empire, to supply a deficiency which may weaken, divide or dissipate the whole?' – 'Their wishes ought to have great weight with him; their opinion, high respect; their business, unremitted attention.' – 'I really think that for wise men this is not judicious; for sober men, not decent; for minds tinctured with humanity, not mild or merciful.' Burke had recourse to this pattern so often that in the end it falls somewhat monotonously on the ear. It has another disadvantage, more noticeable perhaps when read than when heard, that one member of the triad may be so nearly synonymous with another that you cannot but realise that it has been introduced for its sound rather than for its sense.

Burke made frequent use of the antithesis, which of course is merely a variety of balance. Hazlitt says it is first found in *The Tatler*. I have discovered no marked proof of this in an examination which I admit was cursory; there are traces of it, maybe, but adumbrations rather than definite instances. You can find more striking examples in the *Book of Proverbs*. I hazard the guess that it was from this and from his reading of the Latin writers that Johnson developed a device which he made his own. He perfected the form and by his authority gave it a long-continued vogue. The grammars tell us that the antithesis is a mode of structure in which two clauses of a compound sentence are made similar in form, but if this is correct then we must allow two forms of antithesis, the open and the disguised. The open emphasises a contrast, the disguised a balance. Here is an example of an open antithesis: 'The doctor recollected that he had a place to preserve, though he forgot that he had a reputation to lose'; and here is what might be described as a disguised one: 'But if fortune should be as powerful over fame, as she has been prevalent over virtue, at least our conscience is beyond her jurisdiction.'

The antithetical style is vastly effective, and if it has gone out of common use it is doubtless for a reason that Johnson himself suggested. Its purpose is by the balance of words to accentuate the balance of thought, and when it serves merely to tickle the ear it is tiresome. Oddly enough it is just on this account that Coleridge, comparing Johnson's use of it with that of Junius, condemned Johnson: 'the antithesis of Junius,' he said, 'is a real antithesis of images or thought; but the antithesis of Johnson is rarely more than verbal.' It became a trick of phraseology, and with Macaulay, who was the last writer of eminence to practise it, an exasperating trick. It is perhaps a pity that it has gone so completely out of fashion, for it had vigour and cogency. It hit the nail on the head with precision.

The master of the antithesis is the author of the *Letters of Junius*. He wrote admirably. Coleridge, it is true, claimed that when he wrote a sentence of five or six lines long nothing could exceed the slovenliness of his style, a fact which I must confess I have not noticed, but Hazlitt not only admired it, he learnt from it. I will quote the last passage of the letter he addressed to the Duke of Bedford. It is a very good sample of his manner.

'It is in vain therefore to shift the scene. You can no more fly from your enemies than from yourself. Persecuted abroad, you look into your own heart for consolation, and find nothing but reproaches and despair. But, my Lord, you may quit the field of business, though not the field of danger; and though you cannot be safe, you may cease to be ridiculous. I fear you have listened too long to the advice of those pernicious friends, with whose interests you have sordidly united your own, and for whom you have sacrificed everything that ought to be dear to a man of honour. They are still base enough to encourage the follies of your age, as they once did the vices of your youth. As little acquainted with the rules of decorum, as with the laws of morality, they will not suffer you to profit by experience, nor even to consult the propriety of a bad character. Even now they tell you that life is no more than a dramatic scene, in which the hero should preserve his constancy to the last, and that as you lived without virtue you should die without repentance.'

Now, the vogue of the antithesis had a marked effect on sentence structure, as anyone can see for himself by comparing the prose of Dryden, for example, with that of Burke. It brought into prominence the value of the period. I may remind the reader that a period is a sentence in which the sense is held up until the end: when a clause is added after a natural close the sentence is described as loose. The English language does not allow of the inversions which make it possible to suspend the meaning, and so the loose sentence is common. To this is largely due the diffusiveness of our prose. When once the unity of a sentence is abandoned there is little to prevent the writer from adding clause to clause. The antithetical structure was advantageous to the cultivation of the classical period, for it is obvious that its verbal merit depends on its compact and rounded form. I will quote a sentence of Burke's.

'Indeed, when I consider the face of the kingdom of France; the multitude and opulence of her cities; the useful magnificence of her spacious high roads and bridges; the opportunity of her artificial canals and navigations opening the conveniences of maritime communication through a solid continent of so immense an extent; when I turn my eyes to the stupendous works of her ports and harbours, and to her whole naval apparatus, whether for war or trade; when I bring before my view the number of her fortifications, constructed with so bold and masterly a skill, and made and maintained at so prodigious a charge, presenting an armed front and impenetrable barrier to her enemies upon every side; when I recollect how very small a part of that extensive region is without cultivation, and to what complete perfection the culture of many of the best productions of the earth have been brought in France; when I reflect on the excellence of her manufactures and fabrics, second to none but ours, and in some particulars not second; when I contemplate the grand foundations of charity public and private; when I survey the state of all the arts that beautify and polish life; when I reckon the men she has bred for extending her fame in war, her able statesmen, the multitude of her profound lawyers and theologians, her philosophers, her critics, her historians and antiquaries, her poets and her orators, sacred and profane; I behold in all this something which awes and commands the imagination, which checks the mind on the brink of precipitate and indiscriminate censure, and which demands that we should very seriously examine, what and how great are the latent vices that could authorise us at once to level so spacious a fabric with the ground.'

The paragraph ends with three short sentences.

I should like to point out with what skill Burke has given a 'loose' structure to his string of subordinate clauses, thus further suspending the meaning till he brings his period to a close. Johnson, as we know, was apt to make periods of his subordinate clauses, writing what, I think, the grammarians call an extended complex, and so lost the flowing urgency which is characteristic of Burke. I should like to point out also what a happy effect Burke has secured in this compound sentence by forming his different clauses on the same plan and yet by varying cadence and arrangement avoiding monotony. He used the method of starting successive clauses with the same word, in this case with the word *when*, frequently and with effectiveness. It is of course a rhetorical device, which when delivered in a speech must have had a cumulative force, and shows once more how much his style was influenced by the practice of public speaking. I do not know that there is anyone in England who is capable now of writing such a sentence; perhaps there is no one who wants to; for, perhaps from an instinctive desire to avoid the 'loose' sentences which the idiosyncrasy of the language renders so inviting, it is the fashion these days to write short sentences. Indeed not long ago I read that the editor of an important newspaper had insisted that none of his contributors should write a sentence of more than fourteen words. Yet the long sentence has advantages. It gives you room to develop your meaning, opportunity to constitute your cadence and material to achieve your climax. Its disadvantages are that it may be diffuse, flaccid, crabbed or inapprehensible. The stylists of the seventeenth century wrote sentences of great length and did not always escape these defects. Burke seldom failed, however long his sentence, however elaborate its clauses and opulent his 'tropes', to make its fundamental structure so solid that you seem to be led to the safety of the full stop by a guide who knows his business and will permit you neither to take a side-turning nor to loiter by the way. Burke was careful to vary the length of his sentences. He does not tire you with a succession of long ones, nor, unless with a definitely rhetorical intention, does he exasperate you with a long string of short ones.

He has a lively sense of rhythm. His prose has the eighteenth-century tune, like any symphony of Haydn's, though with a truly English accent, and you hear the drums and fifes in it, but an individual note rings through it. It is a virile prose and I can think of no one who wrote with so much force combined with so much elegance. If it seems now a trifle formal, I think that is due to the fact that, like most of the eighteenth-century writers, he used general and abstract terms when we are now more inclined to use special and concrete ones. This gives a greater vividness to modern writing, though at the cost perhaps of concision. It is an amusing exercise to try to translate one of Burke's sentences into such English as the average writer would now write. I have taken one almost at random: 'The tenderest minds, confounded with the dreadful exigence in which morality submits to the suspension of its own rules in favour of its own principles, might turn aside whilst fraud and violence were accomplishing the destruction of a pretended nobility, which disgraced whilst it persecuted, human nature.' It is a fine, rounded period, its meaning is clear and there is not a single word, except perhaps *exigence*, which is not in common use today; yet it is one that smacks of its time, no one would express the thought in such a way now, and in passing I may remark that it is a thought which not a few at the present moment may have had. Perhaps a modern writer would put it somewhat as follows: 'There are times when people even of the most sensitive conscience must put the spirit of the law before the letter, and can do no more than stand aside when an effete plutocracy which has disgraced human nature by its persecutions is destroyed, even though by violence and double dealing.' I do not claim that this is good, it is the best I can do after several attempts and I would not deny that it has neither the balance, the nobility nor the compactness of the original.

Burke was an Irishman, and the Irish, as we know, are inclined to verbosity. With them enough is not as good as a feast. They load their table with sumptuous viands, so that sometimes the mere sight surfeits you, and on occasion even, when you come to attack these game pasties, these boars' heads, these lordly peacocks, you discover to your dismay that like the victuals at a banquet in Italian opera they are of papier mâché. English is a rich language. Very generally you have a choice between a plain word and a literary one, a concrete and an abstract word; you can say a thing directly or you can use a periphrase. The greatness, the stateliness of Burke's nature led him to express himself with grandiloquence. His subjects were important and I suppose he would have thought it unbecoming to them and to himself to deliver himself with simplicity. 'It is very well for Burke to express himself in that figurative way,' said Fox. 'It is natural to him; he talks so to his wife, to his servants, to his children.' It must be admitted that it is sometimes fatiguing. It was not the least of the reasons for his failure in the House of Commons. The greatest speech he ever made there was that on conciliation with the Thirteen States. Lord Morley describes it as 'the wisest in temper, the most closely logical in its reasoning, the amplest in appropriate topics, the most generous and conciliatory in the substance of its appeals.' It drove everybody away.

Dr. Johnson has told us that in his day nobody talked much of style, since everybody wrote pretty well. 'There is an elegance of style universally diffused,' he said. Burke was outstanding. His contemporaries were impressed, as well they might be, by his command of words, his brilliant similes, his hyperboles and fertile imagination, but did not invariably approve. Hazlitt relates a conversation between Fox and Lord Holland on the subject of his style. It appears that this 'Noble Person objected to it as too gaudy and meretricious, and said that it was more profuse of flowers than fruit. On which Mr. Fox observed, that though this was a common objection, it appeared to him altogether an unfounded one; that on the contrary the flowers often concealed the fruit beneath them; and the ornaments of style were rather an hindrance than an advantage to the sentiments they were meant to set off. In confirmation of this remark, he offered to take down the book and translate a page anywhere into his own plain, natural style; and by his doing so, Lord Holland was convinced that he had often missed the thought from having his attention drawn off to the dazzling imagery.' It is instructive to learn that Noble Persons and Eminent Politicians were interested in such questions in those bygone days and with such amiable exercises beguiled their leisure. But of course if his lordship's attention was really drawn off the matter of Burke's discourse by the brillancy of the manner, it is a reflection on his style. For the purpose of imagery is not to divert the reader, but to make the meaning clearer to him; the purpose of simile and metaphor is to impress it on his mind and by engaging his fancy make it more acceptable. An illustration is otiose unless it illustrates. Burke had a romantic and a poetic mind such as no other of the eighteenth-century masters of prose possessed, and it is this that gives his prose its variegated colour; but his aim was to convince rather than to please, to overpower rather than to persuade, and by all the resources of his imagination not only to make his point more obvious, but by an appeal to sentiment or passion to compel acquiescence. I don't know when Mr. Fox held his conversation with the Noble Lord, but if the *Reflections on the French Revolution* had then appeared he might well have pointed to it to refute his lordship's contention. For in that work the decoration so interpenetrates the texture of the writing that it becomes part and parcel of the argument. Here imagery, metaphor and simile fulfil their function. The one passage that leaves me doubtful is the most celebrated of all, that in which Burke tells how he saw Marie Antoinette at Versailles: 'and surely never lighted on this orb, which she hardly seemed to touch, a more delightful vision.' It is to be found in anthologies, so I will not quote it, but it is somewhat high flown to my taste. But if it is not perfect prose it is magnificent rhetoric; magnificent even when it is slightly absurd: 'I thought ten thousand swords must have leapt from their scabbards to avenge even a look that threatened her with insult'; and the cadence with which the paragraph ends is lovely: 'The unbought grace of life, the cheap defence of nations, the nurse of manly sentiment and heroic enterprise is gone! It is gone, that sensibility of principle, that chastity of honour, which felt a stain like a wound, which inspired courage whilst it mitigated ferocity, which ennobled whatever it touched, and under which vice itself lost half its evil, by losing all its grossness.'

Sir Philip Francis, who was perhaps the author of the *Letters of Junius*, condemned this passage as 'downright foppery' and somewhat surprisingly went on to write: 'Once for all I wish you would let me teach you to write English. To me, who aim to read everything you write, it would be a great comfort, and to you, no sort of disparagement. Why will you not allow yourself to be persuaded that polish is material to preservation?'

As the quotations I have given plainly show, Burke made abundant use of metaphor. It is interwoven in the substance of his prose as the weavers of Lyons thread one colour with another to give a fabric the shimmer of shot silk. Of course like every other writer he uses what Fowler calls the natural metaphor, for common speech is largely composed of them, but he uses freely what Fowler calls the artificial metaphor. It gave concrete substance to his generalisations. He used it to enforce a statement by means of a physical image; but unlike some modern writers, who will pursue the implications of a metaphor like a spider scurrying along every filament of its web, he took care never to run it to death. Here is a good example of his practice: 'Your constitution, it is true, whilst you were out of possession, suffered waste and dilapidation; but you possessed in some parts the walls, and, in all, the foundations, of a noble and venerable castle. You might have repaired those walls; you might have built on those foundations.'

On the other hand Burke used the simile somewhat sparingly. Modern writers might well follow his example. For of late a dreadful epidemic has broken out. Similes are clustered on the pages of our young authors as thickly as pimples on a young man's face, and they are as unsightly. A simile has use. By reminding you of a familiar thing it enables you to see the subject of the comparison more clearly or by mentioning an unfamiliar one it focuses your attention on it. It is dangerous to use it merely as an ornament; it is detestable to use it to display your cleverness; it is preposterous to use it when it neither decorates nor impresses. (Example: 'The moon like a huge blancmange wobbled over the tree-tops.') When Burke used a simile it was generally, as might be expected, with elaboration. Here is the most celebrated one: 'But as to *our* country and *our* race, as long as the well-compacted structure of our church and state, the sanctuary, the holy of holies of that ancient law, defended by reverence, defended by power – a fortress at once and a temple – shall stand inviolate on the brow of the British Sion, as long as the British Monarchy – not more limited than fenced by the orders of the state – shall, like the proud Keep of Windsor, rising in the majesty of proportion, and girt with the double belt of its kindred coeval towers; as long as this awful structure shall oversee and guard the subjected land, so long the mounds and dykes of the low, fat, Bedford level will have nothing to fear from all the pickaxes of all the levellers of France.'

Few of us writers pay much attention to the paragraph; we are apt, regardless of the sense, to make a break when we feel the reader deserves the slight rest it gives him. But the extent of a paragraph should be determined not by its length, but by its burden. A paragraph is a collection of sentences with unity of purpose. It should be concerned with a single topic and contain nothing irrelevant to this. Just as in a 'loose' sentence qualifying statements should not overweight the statement qualified, so in the paragraph statements which are of less import should be subordinate to the statement which is essential. Such are the counsels of perfection given by the grammarian. Burke followed them with considerable fidelity. In his best paragraphs he begins with a statement of his subject in short sentences that arrest attention; goes on with a series of sentences of medium length or with a great, majestic period; the phrases grow ampler and more emphatic till he reaches his climax about the middle of the paragraph, or a little later; then he slows down, the sentences grow shorter, sometimes even abrupt, and he concludes.

I have harped upon the fact that Burke's style owed many of its merits to his practice of speaking in public; to this it owed also such defects as a carping critic might find in it. There is more than one passage in the famous speech on the Nabob of Arcot's Debts when he asks a long series of rhetorical questions. It may have been effective in the House of Commons, but on the printed page it is restless and fatiguing. To this may be ascribed his too frequent recourse to the exclamatory sentence. 'Happy if they had all continued to know their indissoluble union, and their proper place! Happy if learning, not debauched by ambition, had been satisfied to continue the instructor, and not aspired to be the master.' Something of an old-fashioned air he has by his frequent use of an inverted construction, a mode now seldom met with; he employs it to vary the monotony of the simple order – subject, verb, object – and also to emphasise the significant member of the sentence by placing it first; but such a phrase as 'Personal offence I have given them none' needs the emphasis of the living voice to appear natural. On the other hand it is to his public speaking, I think, that Burke owed his skill in giving to a series of quite short sentences as musical a cadence and as noble a ring as when he set himself to compose an elaborate period with its pompous train of subordinate clauses; and this is shown nowhere to greater advantage than in the *Letter to a Noble Lord*. Here a true instinct made him see that when he was appealing for compassion on account of his age and infirmities and by reminding his readers of the death of his beloved and only son, he must aim at simplicity. The passage is deeply moving:

'The storm has gone over me; and I lie like one of those old oaks which the late hurricane has scattered about me. I am stripped of all my honours, I am torn up by the roots, and lie prostrate on the earth ... I am alone. I have none to meet my enemies in the gate. Indeed, my lord, I greatly deceive myself, if in this hard season I would give a peck of refuse wheat for all that is called fame and honour in the world. This is the appetite but of a few. It is a luxury, it is a privilege, it is an indulgence for those who are at their ease. But we are all of us made to shun disgrace, as we are made to shrink from pain, and poverty, and disease. It is an instinct; and under the direction of reason, instinct is always in the right. I live in an inverted order. They who ought to have succeeded me have gone before me. They who should have been to me as posterity are in the place of ancestors. I owe to the dearest relation (which ever must subsist in memory) that act of piety, which he would have performed to me; I owe it to him to show that he was not descended, as the Duke of Bedford would have it, from an unworthy parent.'

Here the best words are indeed put in the best places. This piece owes little to picturesque imagery, nothing to romantic metaphor, and proves with what justification Hazlitt described him as, with the exception of Jeremy Taylor, the most poetical of prose-writers. I hope it will not be considered a literary conceit (a trifling, tedious business) when I suggest that in the tender melody of these cadences, in this exquisite choice of simple words, there is a foretaste of Wordsworth at his admirable best. If these pages should persuade anyone to see for himself how great a writer Burke was I cannot do better than advise him to read this *Letter to a Noble Lord*. It is the finest piece of invective in the English language and so short that it can be read in an hour. It offers in its brief compass a survey of all Burke's dazzling gifts, his formal as well as his conversational style, his gift for epigram and for irony, his wisdom, his sense, his pathos, his indignation and his nobility.

Reflections on a Certain Book

I

Punctually at five minutes to five Lampe, his servant, waked Professor Kant and by five, in his slippers, dressing-gown and night-cap, over which he wore his three-cornered hat, he seated himself in his study ready for breakfast. This consisted of a cup of weak tea and a pipe of tobacco. The next two hours he spent thinking over the lecture he was to deliver that morning. Then he dressed. The lecture room was on the ground floor of his house. He lectured from seven till nine and so popular were his lectures that if you wanted a good seat you had to be there by six-thirty. Kant, seated behind a little desk, spoke in a conversational tone, in a low voice, and very rarely indulged in gesture, but he enlivened his discourse with humour and abundant illustrations. His aim was to teach his students to think for themselves and he did not like it when they busied themselves with their quills to write down his every word.

'Gentlemen, do not scratch so,' he said once. 'I am no oracle.'

It was his custom to fix his eyes on a student who sat close to him and judge by the look on his face whether or no he understood what he said. But a very small thing distracted him. On one occasion he lost the thread of his discourse because a button was wanting on the coat of one of the students, and on another when a sleepy youth persistently yawned he broke off to say:

'If one cannot avoid yawning, good manners require that the hand should be placed before the mouth.'

At nine o'clock Kant returned to his room, once more put on his dressing-gown, his night-cap, his three-cornered hat and his slippers and studied till exactly a quarter to one. Then he called down to his cook, told her the hour, dressed and went back to his study to await the guests he expected to dinner. There were never less than two nor more than five. He could not bear to eat alone and it is related that once when it happened that he had no one to bear him company he told his servant to go out into the street and bring in anyone he could find. He expected his cook to be ready and his guests to arrive punctually. He was in the habit of inviting them on the day he wished them to come so that they might not, to dine with him, be tempted to break a previous engagement; and though a certain Professor Kraus for some time dined with him every day but Sunday he never failed to send him an invitation every morning.

As soon as the guests were assembled Kant told his servant to bring the dinner and himself went to fetch the silver spoons which he kept locked up with his money in a bureau in the parlour. The party seated themselves in the dining-room and with the words: 'Now, gentlemen,' Kant set to. The meal was substantial. It was the only one he ate in the day, and consisted of soup, dried pulse with fish, a roast, cheese to end with and fruit when in season. Before each guest was placed a pint bottle of red wine and a pint bottle of white so that he could drink whichever he liked.

Kant was fond of talking, but preferred to talk alone, and if interrupted or contradicted was apt to show displeasure; his conversation, however, was so agreeable that none minded if he monopolised it. In one of his books he wrote: 'If a young, inexperienced man enters a company (especially when ladies are present) surpassing in brilliance his expectations, he is easily embarrassed when he is to begin to speak. Now, it would be awkward to begin with an item of news reported in the paper, for one does not see what led him to speak of that. But as he has just come from the street, the bad weather is the best introduction to conversation.' Though at his own table ladies were never present, Kant made it a rule to start the conversation with this convenient topic; then he turned to the news of the day, home news and foreign, and from this went on to discourse of travellers' tales, and peculiarities of foreign peoples, general literature and food. Finally he told humorous stories, of which he had a rich supply and which he told uncommonly well, so, he said, 'that the repast may end with laughter, which is calculated to promote digestion.' He liked to linger over dinner and the guests did not rise from table till late. He would not sit down after they had left in case he fell asleep and this he would not permit himself to do since he was of opinion that sleep should be enjoyed sparingly, for thus time was saved and so life lengthened. He set out on his afternoon walk.

He was a little man, barely five feet tall, with a narrow chest and one shoulder higher than the other, and he was thin almost to emaciation. He had a crooked nose, but a fine brow and his colour was fresh. His eyes, though small, were blue, lively and penetrating. He was natty in his dress. He wore a small blond wig, a black tie, and a shirt with ruffles round the throat and wrists; a coat, breeches and waistcoat of fine cloth, grey silk stockings and shoes with silver buckles. He carried his three-cornered hat under his arm and in his hand a gold-headed cane. He walked every day, rain or fine, for exactly one hour, but if the weather was threatening, his servant walked behind him with a big umbrella. The only occasion on which he is known to have omitted his walk is when he received Rousseau's *Emile*, and then, unable to tear himself away from it, he remained indoors for three days. He walked very slowly because he thought it was bad for him to sweat, and alone because he had formed the habit of breathing through his nostrils, since thus he thought to avoid catching cold and, had he had a companion with whom courtesy would oblige him to speak, he would have been constrained to breathe through his mouth. He invariably took the same walk, along the Linden Allee, and this, according to Heine, he strolled up and down eight times. He issued from his house at precisely the same hour, so that the people of the town could set their clocks by it. When he came home he returned to his study and read and wrote letters till the light failed. Then, as was his habit, fixing his eyes on the tower of a neighbouring church, he pondered over the problems that just then occupied him. A story is attached to this: it appears that one evening he noticed that he could no longer see the tower, for some poplars had grown so tall that they hid it. It completely upset him, but fortunately the owners of the poplars consented to cut off their tops so that he could continue to reflect in comfort. At a quarter to ten he suspended his arduous labour and by ten was safely tucked up in bed.

But one day somewhere between the middle and the end of July, in the year 1789, when Kant stepped out of his house to take his afternoon walk, instead of turning towards the Linden Allee he took another direction. The inhabitants of Königsberg were astounded and they said to one another that something must have happened in the world of shattering consequence. They were right. He had just received the news that on the fourteenth of July the Paris mob had stormed the Bastille and released the prisoners. It was the beginning of the French Revolution.

Kant was born in very humble circumstances. His father, a harness maker, was a man of high character, and his mother a deeply religious woman. Of them he said: 'They gave me a training which in a moral point of view could not have been better, and for which, at every remembrance of them, I am moved with the most grateful emotions.' He might have gone further and said that the rigid pietism of his mother had no small influence on the system of philosophy he eventually developed. He went to school when he was eight and at sixteen entered the University of Königsberg. By then his mother was dead. His father was too poor to provide him with more than board and lodging, and he got through the six years he spent at the university with some financial help from his uncle, a shoemaker, by taking pupils and, unexpectedly enough, by making a certain amount of money through his skill at billiards and at the card game of ombre. When his father died, Kant being then twenty-two, the home, such as it was, broke up. Of the eleven children Frau Kant had borne her husband, five remained alive: the immediate subject of this narrative, a much younger brother and three girls. The girls went into domestic service and two of them eventually married in their own class of life. The boy was taken care of by his uncle, the shoemaker, and Kant, having failed in his application for an assistant's place at a local school, got a succession of jobs as tutor in the families of the provincial gentry. It was by mixing in a society more polite than that in which he was born and brought up that he acquired the good manners and the social grace for which he was afterwards distinguished. He spent nine years thus occupied, and then, having taken his degree, started upon his career as a lecturer at Königsberg. He lived in lodgings and took his meals at eating-houses which he selected on the chance of meeting agreeable company. But he was pernickety. In one of the lodging-houses he was disturbed in his meditations by the crowing of a cock, and though he tried to buy it the owner would not sell and so he had to move elsewhere. He left one eating-house because a fellow guest talked boringly and another because he found himself expected to hold forth on learned subjects, which was the very thing he did not want to do. It was not till after many years that he was well enough off to have a house of his own and a servant to look after him. The house was sparsely furnished and the only picture in it was a portrait of

Rousseau which had been given him by a friend. The walls had been whitewashed, but in time had grown so black from smoke and soot that you could write your name on them; when, however, a visitor once proceeded to do something like this, Kant mildly rebuked him.

'Friend, why will you disturb the ancient rust?' he asked. 'Is not such a hanging, which arose of its own accord, better than one which is purchased?'

Though he lived to be eighty, he never went more than sixty miles away from the town in which he was born. He suffered from frequent indispositions and was seldom free from pain, but he was able by the exertion of his will to turn his attention away from his feelings just as though they did not concern him. 'He was accustomed to say that one should know how to adapt oneself to one's body.' He was of a cheerful disposition, amiable to all, and considerate; but he was punctilious. He expected the same deference to be paid to him as he paid to others. So when his celebrity made people eager to meet him and a common acquaintance tried to arrange that they should do so by inviting him to his own house he would not consent to go till, however distinguished they were, they had paid him a visit of courtesy.

II

I have given this brief account of what sort of a man Kant was, and what sort of life he led, in the hope of sufficiently whetting the readers' interest in this great philosopher to induce him to have patience with me while I submit to him the reflections that have occurred to me during the reading of a book of his with the somewhat forbidding title of the *Critique of the Power of Judgment*. It deals with two subjects, æsthetics and teleology, but I hasten to add that it is only with the first of these, æsthetics, that I propose to concern myself; and that only with diffidence, for I am well aware that it may be thought presumptuous in a writer of fiction to concern himself with such a matter. I do not pretend to be a philosopher, but merely a man who has throughout his life been profoundly interested in art. All I venture to claim is that I know from experience something of the process of creation and as a writer of fiction can look upon the question of beauty, which is of course the subject matter of æsthetics, with impartiality. Fiction is an art, but an imperfect one. The great novels of the world may deal with all the passions to which man is subject, discover the depths of his variable and disconsolate soul, analyse human relations, describe a civilisation or create immortal characters; it is only by a misuse of the word that beauty can be ascribed to them. We writers of fiction must leave beauty to the poets.

But before I begin to speak of Kant's æsthetic ideas I must tell the reader one very odd thing: he appears to have been entirely devoid of æsthetic sensibility. One of his biographers writes as follows: 'He never seemed to pay much attention to paintings and engravings, even of a superior kind. In galleries and rooms containing much admired and highly praised collections, I never noticed that he specially directed his attention to the pictures, or in any way gave evidence of his appreciation of the artist's skill.' He was not what was called in the eighteenth century a man of feeling. Twice he thought seriously of marrying, but he took so long to consider the advantages and disadvantages of the step he had in mind that in the interval one of the young women he had his eye on married somebody else and the other left Königsberg before he reached a decision. I think this argues that he was not in love, for when you are, even if you are a philosopher, you have no difficulty in finding very good reasons for doing what your inclinations prompt. His two married sisters lived in Königsberg. Kant never spoke to them for twenty-five years. The reason he gave for this was that he had nothing to say to them. This seems sensible enough, and though we may deplore his lack of heart, when we remember how often our pusillanimity has led us to rack our brains in the effort to make conversation with persons with whom we have nothing in common but a tie of blood, we cannot but admire his strength of mind. He had intimate acquaintances rather than friends. When they were ill, he did not care to go to see them, but sent every day to enquire after them, and when they died he put them out of his mind with the words: 'Let the dead rest with the dead.' He was neither impulsive nor demonstrative, but he was kindly, within his scanty means generous, and obliging. His intelligence was great, his power of reasoning impressive, but his emotional nature was meagre.

It is all the more remarkable then that, writing on a subject which depends on feeling, he should have said so much that was wise and even profound. He saw, of course, that beauty does not reside in the object. It is the name we give to the specific feeling of pleasure which the object gives us. He saw also that art can give beauty to things which are in nature ugly or displeasing, but he made the reservation, which certain modern painters might well bear in mind, that some things may be so ugly in their representation as to excite disgust. And in suggesting that when experience proves too commonplace the artist by means of his imagination may work up the material he borrows from nature into something that surpasses nature, Kant may almost be supposed to have foreseen the non-representational art of our own day.

Now, the ideas of a philosopher are largely conditioned by his personal characteristics, and, as one might have expected, Kant's approach to the problems of æsthetics is rigidly intellectual. His aim is to prove that the delight we take in beauty is one of mere reflection. It is interesting to see how he sets about doing this. He starts by making a distinction between the agreeable and the beautiful. The pleasure which the beautiful occasions is independent of all interest. The agreeable is what the senses find pleasing in sensation. The agreeable arouses inclination, and inclination is bound up with desire, and so with interest. A trivial illustration may make Kant's point clear: when I look at the Doric temples at Pæstum the pleasure they afford me is quite obviously independent of all interest and so I may safely call them beautiful; but when I look at a ripe peach the pleasure it causes me is not disinterested, for it excites in me a desire to eat it and therefore I am bound to call it no more than agreeable. The senses of men differ and what causes me pleasure may leave you indifferent. Each of us may judge the agreeable according to his own taste and there is no disputing that. The satisfaction it gives is mere enjoyment, and so, states Kant, has no worth. That is a hard saying, which, I think, can only be explained by his conviction that the faculties of the mind alone have real value. But now, since beauty has no connection with sensation (which is bound up with interest) colour, charm and emotion, which are mere matters of sensation and so only cause enjoyment, have nothing to do with it. This of course is rather startling, but why Kant makes a statement at first sight so outrageous is plain. Since the senses of men differ, if the beautiful depends on the senses your judgment and mine are as good as that of anybody else, and æsthetics will not exist. If a judgment of taste, or what, I think, we would now more conveniently call appreciation of the beautiful, is to have any validity it must depend not on anything so capricious as feeling, but on a mental process. When you come to consider an object with a view to deciding its æsthetic value, you must discard everything, its colour, such charm as it has, the emotion it excites in you, and attend only to its form; and if then you become aware of a harmony between your imagination and your understanding (both faculties of the mind) you will receive a sensation of pleasure and be justified in calling the object beautiful.

But then, having performed this singular operation, you may demand that everyone else should agree with you. The judgment that a thing is beautiful, though a subjective judgment since it is based not on a concept, but on the feeling of pleasure it arouses, has universal validity, and you have the right to claim that everyone *ought* to find beautiful what you find beautiful. In fact it is in a way the duty of others to fall in with your judgment. Kant justifies this contention thus: 'For where anyone is conscious that his delight in an object is with him independent of interest, it is inevitable that he should look on the object as one containing a ground of delight for all men. For, since the delight is not based on any inclination of the subject (or on any other deliberate interest), but the subject feels himself completely free in respect of the liking which he accords to the object, he can find as the reason for his delight no personal conditions to which his own subjective self might alone be party. Hence he must regard it as resting on what he may also presuppose in every other person; and therefore he must believe that he has reason for demanding a similar delight from everyone.'

Yet it looks as though Kant had an inkling that this was rather thin. It may even have occurred to him that the imagination and the understanding were in no better case than the senses, for it is obvious that these two faculties of the mind are not the same in all men. There must have been many people in Königsberg who had more imagination than our philosopher, but none who had so solid an understanding. Kant is forced to presuppose that we can only exact from others agreement with our estimate of what is beautiful by a sense common to all men. But since he admits almost in the same breath that people are often mistaken in judging that an object is beautiful it does not seem to get us much further. And in another place he remarks that an interest in the beautiful is not common: one would have thought that if there were a sense common to all men, all men should be interested in the beautiful. Indeed in the section of his treatise called *Dialectic of Æsthetic Judgment* he states that the only means of saving the claim of the judgment of taste, that is the appreciation of beauty, to universal validity is by supposing a concept of the supersensible lying at the basis of the object and of the judging subject; if I understand aright he means by this that the object of beauty and the person who considers it are both appearances of reality, and reality is one. They are, as it were, a coat and a pair of trousers made out of a bolt of the same fabric. I find this unconvincing. The assumption that in the appreciation of beauty there is a sense common to all men looks to me like nothing more than a futile attempt to prove something that all experience refutes. If the pleasure that is afforded by a beautiful object is subjective, and that of course Kant insists upon, it must depend on the idiosyncrasies of the observer, idiosyncrasies of the mind as well as idiosyncrasies of the senses; and though we, inheritors of Hebraic, Greek and Roman civilisation, have many traits in common we are none of us alike as two peas. Though we may agree more or less on the beauty of certain familiar things, and then perhaps only because they are familiar, it is only natural that our judgments of the beautiful should be as diverse as those of the agreeable admittedly are.

Kant then claimed that when you have decided that an object is beautiful by the process I have just described, you can not only impute the pleasure (a feeling) you experience to everyone else, but also suppose that your pleasure (a feeling, I repeat) is universally communicable. This seems very strange. I should have thought the peculiarity of feeling is that it is not communicable. If I am looking at Giorgione's *Virgin Enthroned* at Castel Franco, I can, if I have any gift of expression, *tell* you what I feel about it, but I cannot make you *feel* my feeling. I can tell you I am in love; I can even describe the feelings that my love excites in me; but I cannot communicate my love, a feeling, to you. If I could you would be in love with the object of my affections, and that might be highly embarrassing to me. Our feelings are surely conditioned by our dispositions. So much is this so that I do not think it an exaggeration to say that no two persons see exactly the same picture or read exactly the same poem. I can only suppose that Kant came by this notion of the universal communicability of feeling owing to his conviction that feeling was negligible except in so far as by means of the imagination and the understanding it gave rise to ideas; and since ideas by the nature of our cognitive faculties *are* universally communicable, the feeling that occasioned them must be so too. He was not, as I ventured at the beginning of this essay to point out, a man who felt with intensity. That may, perhaps, be the reason why he insisted that the appreciation of beauty is merely contemplative.

But contemplation is a passive state. It does not suggest the thrill, the excitement, the breathlessness, the agitation with which the sight of a beautiful picture, the reading of a beautiful poem, must affect a person of æsthetic sensibility. It may well describe his reaction to the agreeable, but surely not to the beautiful. It is difficult for me to believe that any such person can read certain passages of Shakespeare or Milton, listen to certain pieces by Mozart or Beethoven, see certain pictures by El Greco or Chardin with so tepid a feeling that it can be justly called contemplation.

III

Kant's doctrine of the communicability of feeling leads not unnaturally to a consideration of the question of communication. It is obvious that the artist, be he poet, painter or composer, makes a communication, but from

this the writers on æsthetics infer that this is his intention. There I think they are mistaken. They have not
sufficiently examined the process of creation. I don't
believe the artist who sets to work to create a work
of art has any such purpose as they ascribe to him. If
he has he is a didactic or a propagandist, and as such
not an artist. I know what happens to a writer of fiction.
An idea comes to him, he knows not whence, and so
he gives it the rather grand name of inspiration. It is
as slight a thing as the tiny foreign body that finds its
way into the oyster's shell and so creates the disturbance
that will result in the creation of a pearl. For some reason
the idea excites him, his imagination goes to work, out
of his unconscious arise thoughts and feelings, characters
crowd upon him and events suggest themselves that will
express them, for character is expressed by action, not by
description, till at length he is possessed of a shapeless
mass of material. This sometimes, but not always, falls
into a pattern that enables him to see a path, as it were,
which he can follow through the jungle of this confused
medley of feelings and ideas till he is so obsessed by the
muddle of it that to liberate his soul from a burden that
has grown intolerable he is constrained to put it all down
on paper. Having done this he regains his freedom. What
communication the reader gets from it is not his affair.

So it is, I surmise, with the landscape painter, the young
Monet for instance or Pissarro; he cannot tell you why
some scene, the bend of a river, say, or a road under the
snow, bordered by leafless trees, gives him a peculiar thrill
so that the creative instinct is stirred in him and he has
the feeling that here is something that he can deal with,
and because nature has made him a painter he is able
to transmute his emotion into an arrangement of colour
and form that does not satisfy his sensibility, for I think
it doubtful whether the artist, whatever art he practises,
ever achieves the full result he saw in his mind's eye, yet
allays the urge of creation which is at once his delight

143

and his torment. But I do not believe it has ever entered his head that he was making a communication to the persons who afterwards see his picture.

So it is, I submit, with the poet and the composer of music, and if I have spoken of painting rather than of poetry or music it is, frankly, because it is not so difficult to deal with. A picture can be seen at once. Not that I mean a glance will give you all that it has to give. That you can get, if you get it at all, only by giving it your continued and renewed attention. Poetry deals with words and words have overwhelming associations, associations different in different countries and in different cultures. Words affect by their meaning as well as by their sound, and so are addressed to the mind as well as to the sensibility. The only meaning of a picture is the æsthetic delight it gives you. In any case I would not venture to speak of music; the peculiar gift which enables someone to invent it is to me the most mysterious of the processes which produce a work of art. One is taken aback at first to find that Kant placed music (along with cooking) among the inferior arts because, though perhaps the highest among the arts which are valued for their agreeableness, it merely plays with sensation. It was natural that he should do this since he estimated the worth of the arts by the culture they supply to the mind. He has, however, a good word to say of poetry because it gives the imagination an impetus to bring more thought into play than allows of being brought into the embrace of a concept, or therefore being definitely formulated in language; but 'among the formative arts,' he writes, 'I would give the palm to painting because it can penetrate much further into the region of ideas.'

IV

And now, since this does not pretend to be a philosophical dissertation, but merely a discourse on a subject that happens to interest me, I propose to permit myself a digression. The intellectual attitude towards æsthetic appreciation is that of pretty well all the writers on æsthetics. This is perhaps inevitable, for they are compelled to reason about what has little or nothing to do with reason, but almost only with feeling. It was certainly the attitude of Roger Fry. He was a charming man, a lucid writer and an indifferent painter. He rightly earned a high reputation as a critic of art, but, as all but few of us are, he was swayed by certain prejudices of his time. He claimed that a work of art should be conceived in response to a free æsthetic impulse and so condemned the patron unless he allowed the artist to go his own way regardless of the patron's wishes. He had little patience with portraiture because, according to him, people have their portraits painted for social prestige or for purposes of publicity. He regarded the painters who accept such commissions as useless, probably mischievous, parasites upon society. He divided works of art into two distinct classes – 'one in which for some reason the artist can express his genuine æsthetic impulse, the other in which the artist uses his technical skill to gratify a public incapable of responding to æsthetic appeal.' This seems very high-handed. Because the Pharaohs had colossal statues made of themselves presumably with the same intention as Mussolini and Hitler had when they plastered walls with portraits of themselves, namely to impress themselves on the imagination of their subjects, there are Bellini's Doge, Titian's *Man with a Glove*, Velasquez' Pope Innocent, to prove that a portrait can be a work of art and a thing of beauty. We can only suppose that they satisfied their patrons. It is unlikely that had Philip IV been displeased with the portraits Velasquez painted of him, he would have sat to him so often.

The flaw in Roger Fry's argument lies in the presumption that the motives which have led the artist to create a work of art are any business of the critic's or of the layman's. He may, if he is a novelist, start writing a novel to ridicule another novelist, as Fielding started to write *Joseph Andrews* to mock at Richardson, and then, the creative instinct moving him, go on writing for his own enjoyment. Dickens, as we know, was asked to write a book on a subject which did not appeal to him to serve as letterpress for the illustrations of a popular draughtsman and he accepted the commission only because he needed the fourteen pounds a month he was offered for the work. Since he had immense vitality, an exuberant sense of the comic, the power of creating characters as alive as they were fantastic, he produced in *The Pickwick Papers* the greatest work of humour in the English language. It may well be that it was the irksome conditions that he felt bound to accept which gave rise to the flash of genius by means of which, without rhyme or reason, out of the blue, came Sam Weller and Sam Weller's father. It is news to me that the artist who knows his business is hampered by the limitations that are imposed upon him. When the donor of an altarpiece wanted portraits of himself and his wife kneeling at the foot of the Cross with Christ Crucified, perhaps for publicity or for social prestige, but perhaps also because his piety was sincere, in either case the painter had no difficulty in complying with his patron's wish. I cannot believe that it ever entered his head that he looked upon this as an infringement of his æsthetic freedom: on the contrary I am more inclined to believe that the difficulty he was asked to cope with excited and inspired him. Every art has its limitations and the better the artist the more comfortably does he exercise his creative instincts within them.

A generation or two ago a claim was made that painting was an esoteric business that only painters could adequately appreciate since they alone knew its technique. This claim, probably first made in France, where during the last hundred years most æsthetic ideas have arisen, was launched in England, I believe, by Whistler. He asserted that the layman was by his nature a Philistine, and his duty was to accept what the artist oracularly told him. His only function was to buy the painter's picture in order to provide him with bread and butter, but his appreciation was as impertinent as his censure. That was a farrago of nonsense. There is nothing mystical about technique; it is merely the name given to the processes by means of which the artist achieves the effects he aims at. Every art has its technique. It has nothing to do with the layman. He is only concerned with the result. When you look at a picture, if you are of a curious turn of mind it may interest you to examine the way in which the painter has achieved integration through relations of colour, light, line and space; but that is not the æsthetic communication which it has to give you. You do not look at a picture only with your eyes, you look at it with your experience of life, your instinctive likes and dislikes, your habits and feelings, your associations, in fact with the whole of your personality. And the richer your personality the richer is the communication the picture has to give you. The notion, foolish to my mind, that painting is a mystery accessible only to the initiated, is flattering to the painters. It has led them to be scornful of the writers on art who see in pictures what from their professional standpoint is of no interest. I think they are wrong. Leonardo's *Mona Lisa* is not a picture that everyone can care for now, but we know the communication it had to make to Walter Pater; it was not a purely æsthetic communication, but it is surely not the least of this particular picture's merits that it had it to make to a man of peculiar sensibility.

There is a painting by Degas in the Louvre which is popularly known as *L'Absinthe*, but in fact represents an engraver well-known in his day and an actress called Ellen André. There is no reason to suppose that they were more disreputable than other persons of their calling. They are seated side by side at a marble-topped table in a shabby *bistro*. The surroundings are sordid and vulgar. A glass of absinthe stands before the actress. Their dress is slovenly and you can almost smell the stench of their unwashed bodies and grubby clothes. They are slumped down on the *banquette* in an alcoholic stupor. Their faces are heavy and sullen. There is an air of apathetic hopelessness in their listless attitude and you would say that they were dully resigned to sink deeper and deeper into shameless degradation. It is not a pretty picture, nor a pleasing one, and yet it is surely one of the great pictures of the world. It offers the authentic thrill of beauty. Of course I can see how admirable the composition is, how pleasing the colour and how solid the drawing, but to me there is much more in it than that. As I stand before it, my sensibilities quickened, at the back of my mind, somewhere between the conscious and the subconscious, I become aware of Verlaine's poems, and of Rimbaud's, of *Manette Salomon*, of the *quais* along the Seine with their second-hand book-stalls, of the Boulevard St. Michel and the cafés and *bistros* in old mean streets. I dare say that from the standpoint of æsthetic appreciation, which should be occupied only with æsthetic values, this is reprehensible. Why should I care? My delight in the picture is enormously increased. Is it possible that a picture which gives one so much can have been painted, as the distinguished critic, Camille Mauclair, says it was, because Degas was fascinated by the paradoxical perspective of the marble-topped tables in the foreground?

But now I must break off to make a confession to the reader. I have glibly used the word *Beauty* as though I knew just what it meant. I'm not at all sure that I do. It obviously means something, but exactly what? When we say that something is beautiful can we really say why we say it? Do we mean anything more than that it happens to give us a peculiar feeling? I have noticed that the word has bothered the writers on æsthetics not a little; some indeed have sought to avoid it altogether. Some have claimed that it resides in harmony, symmetry and formal relations. Others have identified it with truth and goodness; others again have held that it is merely that which is pleasant. Kant has given several definitions of it, but they all tend to substantiate his claim that the pleasure which beauty affords us is a pleasure of reflection. For all I have been able to discover to the contrary he seems to have believed that beauty was immutable, a belief, I think, generally shared by the writers on æsthetics. Keats expressed the same idea in the first line of *Endymion*: 'A thing of beauty is a joy for ever.' By this he may have meant one of two things: one, that so long as an object retains its beauty it is a pleasure; but that is what I believe philosophers call an analytical proposition, and tells us nothing that we didn't know before, since the characteristic of beauty is that it affords pleasure. Keats was too intelligent to make a statement so trite and I can only think he meant that a thing of beauty is a joy for ever because it retains its beauty for ever. And there he was wrong. For beauty is as transitory as all other things in this world. Sometimes it has a long life, as Greek sculpture has had owing to the prestige of Greek culture and owing to its representations of the human form which have provided us with an ideal of human beauty; but even Greek sculpture, owing to the acquaintance we have now made with Chinese and Negro art, has with the artists themselves lost much of its appeal. It is no longer a source of inspiration. Its beauty is dying. An indication of this may be seen in the movies. Directors no longer choose their heroes as they did twenty years ago for their classical beauty, but for their expression and such evidence as their outward seeming offers of character and personality. They would not do this unless they had discovered that classical beauty had lost its allure. Sometimes the life of beauty is short. We can all remember pictures and poems which gave us the authentic thrill of beauty in our youth, but from which beauty has now seeped out as water seeps out of a porous jar.

Beauty depends on the climate of sensibility and this changes with the passing years. A different generation has different needs and demands a different satisfaction. We grow tired of something we know too well and ask for something new. The eighteenth century saw nothing in the paintings of the Italian Primitives but the fumblings of immature, unskilful artists. Were those pictures beautiful then? No. It is we who have given them their beauty and it is likely enough that the qualities we find in them are not the qualities which appealed to the lovers of art, long since dead, who saw them when they were first painted. Sir Joshua Reynolds, in his *Second Discourse*, recommended Ludovico Caracci as a model for style in painting, in which he thought he approached the nearest to perfection. 'His unaffected breadth of light and shadow,' he said, 'the simplicity of colouring, which, holding its proper rank, does not draw aside the least part of the attention from the subject, and the solemn effect of that twilight which seems diffused over his pictures, appear to me to correspond with grave and dignified subjects, better than the more artificial brilliancy of sunshine which enlightens the pictures of Titian.' Hazlitt was a great critic and enough of a painter to paint a tolerable portrait of Charles Lamb. Of Correggio he wrote that he 'possessed a greater variety of excellence in the different departments of his art than any other painter.' 'Who can think of him,' he asks rhetorically, 'without a swimming of the head?' We can. Hazlitt considered Guercino's *Endymion* one of the finest pictures in Florence. I doubt whether anyone today would give it more than a passing glance. Now, it is no good saying that these eminent persons didn't know what they were talking about; they expressed the cultivated æsthetic opinions of their time. Beauty in fact is only that which produces the specific pleasure which leads us to describe an object as beautiful during a certain period of the world's history, and it does so because it responds to certain needs of the period. It would be foolish to suppose that our opinions are any more definitive than those of our fathers, and we may be pretty sure that our descendants will look upon them with the same perplexity as we look upon Sir Joshua's high praise of Pellegrino Tibaldi and Hazlitt's passionate admiration for Guido Reni.

V

I have suggested that there is between the creation of beauty and the appreciation of it a disjunction which no bridge can span, and from what I have said the reader will have gathered that I think the appreciation is enhanced by, if not actually dependent upon, the culture of the individual. That is what the connoisseurs of art and the lovers of beauty claim, and they claim also that the gift of æsthetic appreciation is a rare one. If they are right it demolishes Tolstoi's contention that real beauty is accessible to everyone. Perhaps the most interesting part of Kant's *Critique of Æsthetic Judgment* is the long section he devotes to the sublime. I need only trouble the reader with his conclusions. He points out that the peasant who lives among mountains merely looks upon them as horrible and dangerous (as we know the ancient travellers did) and the sea-faring man looks upon the sea as a treacherous and uncertain element which it is his business to contend with. To receive from the snow-clad mountains and the stormtossed sea the specific pleasure which we call the sublime demands a susceptibility to ideas and a certain degree of culture. That has an air of truth. Is the farmer conscious of the beauty of the landscape in the sight of which he earns his daily bread? I should say not; and that is natural, for the appreciation of beauty, it is agreed, must not be affected by practical considerations, and he is concerned to plough a field or to dig a ditch. The appreciation of the beauty of nature is a recent acquisition of the human race. It was created by the painters and writers of the Romantic Era. It needs leisure and sophistication. In order to appreciate it, then, not only disinterestedness is needed, but culture and a susceptibility to ideas. Unwelcome as the idea may be, I don't see how one can escape admitting that beauty is accessible but to the chosen few.

But to admit that excites in me a feeling of deep discomfort. More than twenty-five years ago I bought an abstract picture by Fernand Léger. It was an arrangement of squares, oblongs and spheres in black, white, grey and red, and for some reason he had called it *Les Toits de Paris*. I did not think it beautiful, but I found it ingenious and decorative. I had a cook then, a bad-tempered and quarrelsome woman, who would stand looking at this picture for quite long periods in a state of something that looked very like rapture. I asked her what she saw in it. 'I don't know,' she answered, '*mais ça me plaît, ça me dit quelque chose.*' It seemed to me that she was receiving as genuine an æsthetic emotion as I flattered myself I received from El Greco's *Crucifixion* in the Louvre. I am led by this (a single instance, of course) to suggest that it is a very narrow point of view which claims that the specific pleasure of artistic appreciation can only be felt by the privileged few. It may well be that the pleasure is subtler, richer and more discriminating in someone whose personality is cultivated, whose experience is wide, but why should we suppose that someone else, less fortunately circumstanced, cannot feel a pleasure as intense and as fruitful? The object that in the latter gives rise to the pleasure may be what the æsthete considers no great shakes. Does that matter? It appears that the urn which inspired Keats to write his great ode was a mediocre piece of Greco-Roman sculpture, yet it gave him the æsthetic thrill which, being what he was, occasioned one of the most beautiful poems in the English language. Kant put the matter succinctly when he said that beauty does not reside in the object. It is the name we give to the specific pleasure which the object gives us. Pleasure is a feeling I can see no reason why there should not be as many people capable of enjoying the specific pleasure of beauty as there are who are capable of feeling grief or joy, love, tenderness and compassion. I am inclined to say that Tolstoi was right when he said that real beauty is accessible to everyone if you leave out the word *real*. There is no such thing as real beauty. Beauty is what gives you and me and everyone else that sense of exultation and liberation which I have already spoken of. But in discourse it is more convenient to use the word as if it were a material entity, like a chair or a table, existing in its own right, independent of the observer, and that I shall continue to do.

VI

Now, after this long digression from my subject, which is Kant's æsthetic ideas, I must attempt to cope with what I have found the most difficult part of his treatise, and that is his discussion of purposiveness and purpose in relation to beauty. And what makes it more difficult is that he seems sometimes to use the two words as though they were synonymous. (The German words are *Zweck* and *Zweckmässigkeit*.) In this essay, designed to interest the general reader, I have been at pains to avoid the technical terms of philosophy, but now I must ask his indulgence while I give him Kant's definition of purpose and purposiveness. It runs as follows: 'Purpose is the object of a concept in so far as this concept is regarded as the cause of the object, that is to say as the real ground of its possibility. The causality of a concept in respect of its object is its purposiveness.' Kant gives an illustration which makes the matter clear: a man builds a house in order to rent it. That is his purpose in building it. But the house would not have been built at all unless he had conceived the idea that he would receive rent from it. This concept is the purposiveness of building the house. There is a certain humour, probably unconscious, in one example which our philosopher gives of purposiveness in nature: 'The vermin that torment men in their clothes, their hair, or their bed may be according to a wise appointment of nature a motive of cleanliness which is in itself an important means for the preservation of health.' But that these vermin have been created for this purpose cannot be a conviction, but at most a persuasion. It may be no more than a wholesome illusion. The purposiveness which we seem to find in nature may be occasioned only by the peculiar constitution of our cognitive faculties. It is a principle we make use of to provide ourselves with concepts in the vast multiplicity of nature, so that we may take our bearings in it and enable our understanding to feel itself at home in it.

Fortunately for myself I am only concerned with this principle in so far as it is related to Kant's æsthetic ideas. Beauty, he states, is the form of purposiveness in an object so far as it is perceived in it apart from the representation of a purpose. This purposiveness, however, is not real; we are forced by the subjective needs of our nature to ascribe it to the object which we call beautiful. Since I am more at ease with the concrete than with the abstract I have tried to think of an object of beauty which has purposiveness apart from purpose, and that is not so easy since the simplest definition of purposiveness is that it is characterised by purpose. I offer an illustration with diffidence. A rice bowl of the Yung Lo period, of the porcelain known as eggshell, is so wafer-thin, so fragile, so delicate in texture that its purpose is evidently not to contain rice. Such a purpose would be of practical interest and the appreciation of beauty is essentially disinterested. Furthermore, there is an admirably drawn design under the glaze which can only be seen when you hold the bowl, empty, up to the light. What other purposiveness can it have but to please the eye? But if by the purposiveness of an object of beauty Kant had merely meant that it affords pleasure he would surely have said so. I have an inkling that at the back of his great mind was a disinclination to admit that pleasure was the only effect to be obtained from the consideration of a great work of art.

Pleasure has always had a bad name. Philosophers and moralists have been unwilling to own that it is good and only to be eschewed when its consequences are harmful. Plato, as we know, condemned art unless it led to right action. Christianity with its contempt of the body and its obsession with sin viewed pleasure with apprehension and its pursuit unworthy of a human being with an immortal soul. I suppose that the disapproval with which pleasure is regarded arises from the fact that when people think of it, it is in connection with the pleasures of the body. That is not fair. There are spiritual pleasures as well as physical pleasures, and if we must allow that sexual intercourse, as St. Augustine (who knew something about it) declared, is the greatest of physical pleasures, we may admit that æsthetic appreciation is the greatest of spiritual pleasures.

Kant says that the artist produces a work of art with no other purpose than to make it beautiful. I do not believe that is so; I believe that the artist produces a work of art to exercise his creative faculty, and whether what he creates is beautiful is a fortuitous result in which he may well be uninterested. We know from Vasari that Titian was a fashionable and prolific portrait painter. His experience was wide and he knew his business, so that when he came to paint the *Man with a Glove* it is probable enough that he was concerned only to get a good likeness and satisfy his client. It was a happy accident that, owing to his own great gifts and the natural grace of his sitter, he achieved beauty. Milton has concisely told us what his purpose was in writing *Paradise Lost*, it was a didactic purpose, and if in passage after passage he achieved beauty I cannot but think that this too was a happy accident. It may be that beauty, like happiness and originality, is more likely to be obtained when it is not deliberately attempted.

I have not thought it necessary in this discourse to touch upon Kant's discussion of the sublime, though, as he insists, our judgments about the beautiful and the sublime are akin, since both are æsthetic judgments. The purposiveness we are obliged to ascribe to both (unfortunately Kant does not tell us why) is entirely subjective. 'We call things sublime', he says, 'on the ground that they make us feel the sublimity of our own minds.' Our imagination cannot cope with the feeling that arises in us when we contemplate the raging, storm-tossed sea and the massed immensities of the Himalayas, with their eternal snows. We are made to feel our insignificance, but at the same time we are exalted, since, awe-struck as we may be, we are conscious that we are not limited to the world of sense, but can raise ourselves above it. 'Nature may deprive us of everything, but it has no power over our moral personality.' So Pascal said: *'L'homme n'est qu'un roseau, le plus foible de la nature, mais c'est un roseau pensant, il ne faut pas que l'Univers entier s'arme pour l'écraser, une vapeur, une goutte d'eau suffit pour le tuer. Mais quand l'Univers l'écraserait, l'homme serait encore plus noble que ce qui le tue, parce qu'il scait qu'il meurt et l'avantage que l'Univers a sur lui, L'Univers n'en scait rien.'* If Kant had had the æsthetic sensibility which, as I remarked early in this essay, he seems singularly to have lacked, it might perhaps have occurred to him that the emotions we feel, and the ideas that spring from them, when we contemplate a supreme work of art, the ceiling of the Sistine Chapel or El Greco's *Crucifixion* in the Louvre, are not so very different from those we have when we are confronted with the objects we describe as sublime. They are moral emotions and moral ideas.

Kant, as we know, was a moralist. 'Reason,' he says, 'can never be persuaded that the existence of a man who merely lives for enjoyment has worth in itself.' That we may all agree to. Then he says: 'If the beautiful arts are not brought into more or less combination with moral ideas ... they serve only as a distraction, of which we are the more in need the more we avail ourselves of them to disperse the discontent of the mind with itself, so that we render ourselves ever more useless and more discontented.' He goes even further when at the very end of his treatise he says that the true introduction to the appreciation of beauty is the development of the moral ideas and the culture of moral feeling. It is not for me who am no philosopher to suggest that by his difficult proposition that beauty is the form of the purposiveness of an object so far as this is perceived without any presentation of a purpose, Kant may have meant something other than what he said, but, I must confess, it seems to me that if the purposiveness which we are apparently forced to ascribe to the work of art lies only in the artist's intention these scattered observations of his are somewhat pointless; for what has the artist's intention to do with us? We, I repeat, are only concerned with what he has done.

Jeremy Bentham startled the world many years ago by stating in effect that if the amount of pleasure obtained from each be equal there is nothing to choose between poetry and push-pin. Since few people now know what push-pin is, I may explain that it is a child's game in which one player tries to push his pin across that of another player, and if he succeeds and then is able by pressing down on the two pins with the ball of his thumb to lift them off the table he wins possession of his opponent's pin. When I was a small boy at a preparatory school we used to play it with steel nibs till the headmaster discovered that we had somehow turned it into a gambling game, whereupon he forbade us to play it, and when he caught us still doing so, soundly beat us. The indignant retort to Bentham's statement was that spiritual pleasures are obviously higher than physical pleasures. But who say so? Those who prefer spiritual pleasures. They are in a miserable minority, as they acknowledge when they declare that the gift of æsthetic appreciation is a very rare one. The vast majority of men are, as we know, both by necessity and choice preoccupied with material considerations. Their pleasures are material. They look askance at those who spend their lives in the pursuit of art. That is why they have attached a depreciatory sense to the word æsthete, which means merely one who has a special appreciation of beauty. How are we going to show that they are wrong? How are we going to show that there *is* something to choose between poetry and push-pin? I surmise that Bentham chose push-pin for its pleasant alliteration with poetry. Let us speak of lawn tennis. It is a popular game which many of us can play with pleasure. It needs skill and judgment, a good eye and a cool head. If I get the same amount of pleasure out of playing it as you get by looking at Titian's *Entombment of Christ* in the Louvre, by listening to Beethoven's *Eroica* or by reading Eliot's *Ash Wednesday*, how are you going to prove that your pleasure is better and more refined than mine? Only, I should say, by manifesting that this gift you have of æsthetic appreciation has a moral effect on your character.

In one place Kant makes the significant remark that 'connoisseurs in taste, not only often, but generally are given up to idle, capricious and mischievous passions' and that 'they could perhaps make less claims than others to any superiority of attachment to moral principles.' This was doubtless true then: it is true now. Human nature changes little. No one can have lived much in the society of those whom Kant calls connoisseurs of taste, and whom we may more conveniently call æsthetes, without noticing how seldom it is that you find in them the modesty, the tolerance, the loving-kindness and liberality, in short the goodness with which you might have expected their addiction to spiritual pleasures to inform them. If the delight in æsthetic appreciation is no more than the opium of an intelligentsia it is no more than, as Kant says, a mischievous distraction. If it is more it should enable its possessor to acquire virtue. Kant finely says that beauty is the symbol of morality. Unless the love of beauty ennobles the character, and that is the only purposiveness of beauty that seems, as far as I can see, important enough to give it value, then I can't tell how we can escape from Bentham's affirmation that if the amount of pleasure obtained from each be equal there is nothing to choose between poetry and push-pin.

Some Novelists I Have Known

I

One of Hazlitt's most enchanting essays is *My First Acquaintance with Poets*, in which he relates how he came to know Coleridge and Wordsworth. Coleridge had come to Shrewsbury to take charge of its Unitarian Congregation, and Mr. Rowe, whom he was succeeding, went down to the coach to meet him; but though he saw a round-faced man in a short black coat who seemed to be talking at a great rate to his fellow-passengers he could find no one answering the description of the man he was expecting. He went home, but had scarcely got there when the round-faced man in the black coat entered and 'dissipated all doubts on the subject, by beginning to talk. He did not cease while he stayed; nor has he since, that I know of.' Hazlitt's father, a dissenting minister, lived ten miles from Shrewsbury and a few days later Coleridge walked over to see him. Hazlitt, then twenty years old, was presented to him. The poet found the young man an enthusiastic and intelligent listener and invited him to come to Nether-Stowey in the spring. This Hazlitt did, and after he had been there a day or two Wordsworth arrived. 'He instantly began to make havoc of the half of a Cheshire cheese on the table, and said triumphantly that his marriage with experience had not been so unproductive as Mr. Southey's in teaching him a knowledge of the good things of this life.' Next day Coleridge and Hazlitt accompanied Wordsworth to Alfoxden, where he read in the open air the story of Peter Bell. 'There is a charm in the recitation both of Coleridge and Wordsworth,' says Hazlitt, 'which acts as a spell upon the heart, and disarms the judgment. Perhaps they have deceived themselves by making use of this ambiguous accompaniment.' Hazlitt, though excited and admiring, relinquished neither his critical acumen nor his sense of humour.

It is the delight I take in this essay that has prompted me to write the following pages. Alas, I have no such great figures to write about as Coleridge and Wordsworth. *The Ancient Mariner, Kubla Khan,* the great ode and *The Solitary Reaper* will be read as long as English poetry is read; but who can tell whether any of the authors with whom I propose to deal in this essay will be remembered by posterity. Brahma, the Indian monists think, created the world for sport, thus exercising in this little bit of fun the infinite activity which is one of his attributes; and it is with just such sardonic and unscrupulous humour that posterity orders literary fame. Its wilfulness is beyond reason. It takes no account of virtue and little of industry; it is indifferent to high endeavour and sincerity of purpose. How unjust it is that Mrs. Humphry Ward, with her well-stored mind and her command of language, with her solid gifts, her conscientiousness and her seriousness, should be so forgotten that even her name will be unknown to most readers of today, whereas a dissipated French abbé, a hack-writer of the eighteenth century who wrote interminable and unreadable novels, should have achieved immortality because in the long course of one of them he wrote the story of a little baggage called Manon Lescaut.

Before I begin I should like to make it quite clear that though I knew the authors I am going to speak of over a long period I was not really intimate with any of them. One reason of this is that until I made a success as a writer of light comedies I knew very few authors, and for the most part those I knew, and only casually, were like myself very small fry. One's intimate friends are those one makes in one's teens or early twenties. I was thirty-four when I became a popular playwright, and though after that I came in contact with many of the literary figures of the day they were a good deal older than me and they were by then too much occupied with their own activities and the friends these had brought them for me to become anything more than a random acquaintance. I have been a wanderer all my life and when I was not wanted in London for the rehearsals of a play I spent long periods out of England so that I lost touch with the people my success had enabled me to meet.

French authors live for the greater part of the year in Paris. They form cliques and the members of a clique meet constantly, in cafés, in newspaper offices, in their apartments; they dine together and talk and criticise one another's books; they write to one another (with a view to future publication) immense letters. They defend one another; they attack one another. English authors are different. On the whole they are not much interested in their fellow-writers. They are apt to live in the country and only go to London when they need to. They are more indiscriminately social than the French and mix freely in circles other than literary. Their close friends are, as with Henry James, a little group of fervent admirers or, as with H. G. Wells, the persons who share their particular interests. If you are not numbered among one or other of these classes you have little chance of admittance into their intimacy. But the chief reason why I have never become easily familiar with the men of letters I propose to write about is owing to some fault in my own character. I am either too self-centred, or too diffident, or too reserved, or too shy to be able to be on confidential terms with anyone I know at all well, and when on occasion a friend in trouble has opened his heart to me I have been too embarrassed to be of much help to him. Most people like to talk about themselves and when they tell me things I should have thought they would prefer to keep to themselves I am abashed. I prefer to guess at the secrets of their hearts. It is not in me to take people at their face value and I am not easily impressed. I have no power of veneration. It is more in my humour to be amused by people than to respect them.

Many have been on terms of much closer friendship with the more or less illustrious persons my recollections of whom I am now offering to the reader, and I have written the above only to impress upon him that they (my recollections) can suggest no more than a partial portrait of my subjects.

I saw Henry James long before I knew him. Somehow or other I was allotted two seats in the dress circle for the first night of *Guy Domville*. I can't think why, because I was still a medical student and one of George Alexander's first nights was a fashionable affair and seats in the better parts of the house were distributed among critics, regular first-nighters, friends of the management and persons of consequence. The play was a dreadful failure. The dialogue was graceful, but perhaps not quite direct enough to be taken in by an audience and there was a certain monotony in its rhythm. Henry James was fifty when he wrote the play and it is hard to understand how such a practised writer could have invented such a tissue of absurdities as was that night presented to the public. There was in the second act a distressing scene of pretended drunkenness which gave one goose-flesh. One blushed for the author. The play reached its tedious end and Henry James was very unwisely brought on the stage to take a bow, as was the undignified custom of the time. He was greeted with such an outburst of boos and catcalls as only then have I heard in the theatre. From my seat in the dress circle he seemed oddly fore-shortened. A stout man on stumpy legs, and owing to his baldness, notwithstanding his beard, a vast expanse of naked face. He confronted the hostile audience, his jaw fallen so that his mouth was slightly open and on his countenance a look of complete bewilderment. He was paralysed. I don't know why the curtain wasn't immediately brought down. He seemed to stand there interminably while the gallery and the pit continued to bawl. There was clapping in the stalls and dress circle, and he said afterwards that it was enthusiastic, but there he was mistaken. It was half-hearted. People clapped in protest at the rudeness of pit and gallery, and out of pity because they could not bear to see the wretched man's humiliation. At last George Alexander came out and led him, crushed and cowed, away.

In a letter he wrote to his brother William after that disastrous evening Henry James, like many another dramatist who has had a failure, said that his play was 'over the heads of the usual vulgar theatre-going London public'. That was not the fact. It was a bad play. It is possible that the outcry would have been less violent if the audience had not been exasperated by the incredible conduct of the characters. Their motives were, as in so much of Henry James's work, not the motives of normal human beings, and though in his fiction he was persuasive enough very often to conceal the fact from the reader, presented on the stage they glaringly lacked plausibility. The audience felt instinctively that people did not behave with the lack of common sense with which he made them behave and, so feeling, felt that they had been made fools of. In their boos there was more than irritation because they had been bored, there was resentment.

One can see the play Henry James wanted to write and perhaps thought he had written, but it is wretchedly evident that he fell very far short of his intention. He despised the English theatre and was convinced that he could write much better plays himself. Years before in Paris he wrote that he had 'mastered Dumas, Augier and Sardou', and claimed that he knew 'all they knew and a great deal more besides.' Why he failed as a dramatist is obvious enough. He was like a man who because he can ride a bicycle thinks he can ride a horse. If under that impression he goes out for a day with the Pytchley he will come a cropper at the first fence. One unfortunate result of Henry James's misadventure was that it confirmed managers in the belief that no novelist could write a play.

II

It was not till many years later, when I had myself written successful plays, that I met Henry James. It was at a luncheon party given by Lady Russell, the author of *Elizabeth and her German Garden*, in a flat she then had, if I remember rightly, near Buckingham Gate. It was by way of being a literary party and Henry James was of course the lion of the occasion. He said a few polite words to me, but I received the impression that they meant very little. I forget how long it was after this that I happened to go to an afternoon performance of *The Cherry Orchard* given by the Stage Society and found myself sitting next to Henry James and Mrs. W. K. Clifford, the widow of the mathematician, and herself the author of two good novels, *Mrs. Keith's Crime* and *Aunt Anne*. The intervals were long and we had ample time to talk. Henry James was perplexed by *The Cherry Orchard*, as well he might be when his dramatic values were founded on the plays of Alexander Dumas and Sardou, and in the second interval he set out to explain to us how antagonistic to his French sympathies was this Russian incoherence. Lumbering through his tortuous phrases, he hesitated now and again in search of the exact word to express his dismay; but Mrs. Clifford had a quick and agile mind; she knew the word he was looking for and every time he paused immediately supplied it. This was the last thing he wanted. He was too well-mannered to protest, but an almost imperceptible expression on his face betrayed his irritation and, obstinately refusing the word she offered, he laboriously sought another, and again Mrs. Clifford suggested it only to have it again turned down. It was a scene of high comedy.

Ethel Irving was playing the part of Chekov's feckless heroine. She was herself moody, neurotic and emotional, which suited the character, and her performance was excellent. She had made a great success in a play of mine and Henry James was curious to know about her. I told him what I could. Then he put me a very simple question, but he felt it would be crude and perhaps a trifle snobbish to put it simply. Both Mrs. Clifford and I knew exactly what he wanted to say. He led up to his enquiry like a big-game hunter stalking an antelope. He approached stealthily and drew back when he suspected that the shy creature winded him. He wrapped up his meaning in an increasingly embarrassed maze of circumlocution till at last Mrs. Clifford could stand it no longer and blurted out: 'Do you mean, is she a lady?' A look of real suffering crossed his face. Put so, the question had a vulgarity that outraged him. He pretended not to hear. He made a little gesture of desperation and said: 'Is she, *enfin*, what you'd call if you were asked point-blank, if so to speak you were put with your back to the wall, is she a *femme du monde*?'

In 1910 I went to America for the first time and in due course paid a visit to Boston. Henry James, his brother having recently died, was staying at Cambridge, Massachusetts, with his sister-in-law and Mrs. James asked me to dinner. There were but the three of us. I can remember nothing of the conversation, but I could not help noticing that Henry James was troubled in spirit, and after dinner, when the widow had left us alone in the dining-room, he told me that he had promised his brother to remain at Cambridge for, I think, six months after his death, so that if he found himself able to make a communication from beyond the grave there would be two sympathetic witnesses on the spot ready to receive it. I could not but reflect that Henry James was in so nervous a state that it would be difficult to place implicit confidence in any report he might make. His sensibility was so exacerbated that he was capable of imagining anything. But hitherto no message had come and the six months were drawing to their end.

When it was time for me to go Henry James insisted on accompanying me to the corner where I could take the street-car back to Boston. I protested that I was perfectly capable of getting there by myself, but he would not hear of it, not only on account of the kindness and the great courtesy which were natural to him, but also because America seemed to him a strange and terrifying labyrinth in which without his guidance I was bound to get hopelessly lost.

As we walked along, he told me what his good manners had prevented him from saying before Mrs. James, that he was counting the days that must elapse before, having fulfilled his promise, he could sail for the blessed shores of England. He yearned for it. There, in Cambridge, he felt himself forlorn. He was determined never to set foot again on that bewildering and unknown country that America was to him. It was then that he uttered the phrase which seemed to me so fantastic that I have never forgotten it. 'I wander about these great empty streets of Boston,' he said, 'and I never see a soul. I could not be more alone in the Sahara.' The street-car hove in sight and Henry James was seized with agitation. He began waving frantically when it was still a quarter of a mile away. He was afraid it wouldn't stop, and he besought me to jump on with the greatest agility of which I was capable, for it would not pause more than an instant, and if I were not very careful I might be dragged along and if not killed, at least mangled and dismembered. I assured him I was quite accustomed to getting on street-cars. Not American street-cars, he told me, they were of a savagery, an inhumanity, a ruthlessness beyond any conception. I was so infected by his anxiety that when the car pulled up and I leapt on, I had almost the sensation that I had had a miraculous escape from certain death. I saw him standing on his short legs in the middle of the road, looking after the car, and I felt that he was trembling still at my narrow shave.

But homesick as he was for England I don't believe that he ever felt himself quite at home there. He remained a friendly, but critical alien. He did not know the English as an Englishman instinctively knows them and so his English characters never to my mind ring quite true. His American characters, at least to an Englishman, on the whole do. He had certain remarkable gifts, but he lacked the quality of empathy which enables a novelist to feel himself into his characters, think their thoughts and suffer their emotions. Flaubert vomited as though he too had swallowed arsenic when he was describing the suicide of Emma Bovary. It is impossible to imagine Henry James being similarly affected if he had had to narrate a similar episode. Take *The Author of Beltraffio*. In that a mother lets her only child, a little boy, die of diphtheria so that he should not be corrupted by his father's books, of which she profoundly disapproves. No one could have conceived such a monstrous episode who could imagine a mother's love for her son and in his nerves feel the anguish of the child tossing restlessly on his bed and the pitiful, agonising struggle for breath. That is what the French call *littérature*. There is no precise English equivalent. On the pattern of writer's cramp you might call it writer's hokum. It signifies the sort of writing produced purely for literary effect without a relation to truth or probability. A novelist may ask himself what it feels like to commit a murder and then may invent a character who commits one to know what it feels like. That is *littérature*. People commit murders for reasons that seem good to them, not in order to enjoy a curious experience. The great novelists, even in seclusion, have lived life passionately. Henry James was content to observe it from a window. But you cannot describe life convincingly unless you have partaken of it; nor, should your object be different, can you fantasticate upon it (as Balzac and Dickens did) unless you know it first. Something escapes you unless you have been an actor in the tragi-comedy. However realistic he tries to be, the novelist cannot hope to give a representation of life as exactly as a lithograph can give a representation of a drawing. With his characters and the experiences he causes them to undergo he draws a pattern, but he is more likely to convince his readers that the pattern is acceptable if the people he depicts have the same sort of motives, foibles and passions as they know they have themselves and if the experiences of the persons in question are such as their characters render plausible.

Henry James regarded his relations and friends with deep affection, but this is no indication that he was capable of love. Indeed he showed a singular obtuseness in his stories and novels when he came to deal with the most deeply seated of human emotions; so that, interested and amused as you are, (often amused at him rather than with him,) you are constantly jolted back to reality by your feeling that human beings simply do not behave as he makes them do. You cannot take Henry James's fiction quite seriously as, for instance, you take *Anna Karenina* or *Madame Bovary*; you read it with a smile, and with the suspension of disbelief with which you read the Restoration dramatists. (This notion is not so far-fetched as it may seem at first sight: if Congreve had been a novelist he might well have written the bawdy narrative of promiscuous fornication which Henry James entitled *What Maisie Knew.*) There is all the difference between his novels and those of Flaubert and Tolstoi as there is between the paintings of Daumier and the drawings of Constantin Guys. The draughtsman's pretty women drive in the Bois in their smart carriages, luxurious and fashionable, but they have no bodies in their elegant clothes. They amuse, they charm; but they are as unsubstantial as the stuff that dreams are made of. Henry James's fictions are like the cobwebs which a spider may spin in the attic of some old house, intricate, delicate and even beautiful, but which at any moment the housemaid's broom with brutal common sense may sweep away.

It is not my purpose to criticise Henry James's work, yet it is impossible in his case to write of the man rather than of the author. They are in fact inseparable. The author absorbed the man. To him it was art that made life significant, but he cared little for any of the arts except the one he practised. He was little interested in music or painting. When Gosse was going to Venice he conjured him without fail to see Tintoretto's *Crucifixion* at San Cassiano. It is odd that he should have picked out this fine but stagey picture to commend rather than Titian's grand *Presentation of the Virgin* or Veronese's *Jesus in the House of Levi*. No one who knew Henry James in the flesh can read his stories dispassionately. He got the sound of his voice into every line he wrote, and you accept (not willingly, but with indulgence) the abominable style of his later work, with its ugly Gallicisms, its abuse of adverbs, its too elaborate metaphors, the tortuosity of its long sentences, because they are part and parcel of the charm, benignity and amusing pomposity of the man you remember.

I am not sure that Henry James was fortunate in his friends. They were disposed to be possessive, and they regarded one another's claim to be in the inner circle of his confidence with no conspicuous amiability. Like a dog with a bone, each was inclined to growl when another showed an inclination to dispute his exclusive right to the precious object of his devotion. The reverence with which they treated him was of no great service to him. They seemed to me, indeed, sometimes a trifle silly:

they whispered to one another with delighted giggles that Henry James privately stated that the article in *The Ambassadors* on the manufacture of which the fortune of the widow Newsome was founded, and the nature of which he had left in polite obscurity, was in fact a chamber pot. I did not find this so amusing as they did. I think it would be unfair to say that Henry James demanded the admiration of his friends, but he certainly enjoyed it. English authors, unlike their fellows in France and Germany, are chary of assuming an attitude. The pose of *Cher Maire* makes them feel faintly ridiculous. Perhaps because Henry James had first come to know distinguished writers in France he took the pedestal on which his admirers placed him as a natural prerogative. He was touchy and could be cross when he was not treated with what he thought proper respect. On one occasion a young Irish friend of mine was staying at Hill for the week-end in company with Henry James. Mrs. Hunter, their hostess, told him that he was a talented young man and Henry James on the Saturday afternoon engaged him in conversation. My friend was petulant and impatient, and at length, driven to desperation by James's interminable struggle to find the one word that would express exactly what he wanted to say, blurted out: 'Oh, Mr. James, I'm not of any importance. Don't bother about rooting around for the right word. Any old word is good enough for me.' Henry James was deeply affronted and complained to Mrs. Hunter that the young man had been very rude to him, whereupon Mrs. Hunter gave him a severe scolding and insisted that he should apologise to her distinguished guest. This he accordingly did. Once Jane Wells inveigled Henry James and me to go with her to a subscription dance in aid of some worthy object in which H. G. was interested. Mrs. Wells, Henry James and I were chatting in a kind of anteroom adjoining the ballroom when a brash young man bounced in, interrupting Henry James in his discourse, and seizing Jane Wells's hands said: 'Come on and dance, Mrs. Wells, you don't want to sit there listening to that old man talking his head off.' It wasn't very polite. Jane Wells gave Henry James an anxious glance and then with a strained smile went off with the brash young man. Henry James was too little accustomed to be treated like that to take it, as he might sensibly have done, with a good-natured laugh, and he was much offended. When Mrs. Wells came back he got up and a little too formally bade her good-night.

When someone transplants himself from one country to another he is more likely to assimilate the defects of its inhabitants than their virtues. The England in which Henry James lived was excessively class-conscious, and I think it is to this that must be ascribed the somewhat disconcerting attitude he adopted in his fiction to those who were so unfortunate as to be of humble origin. Unless he were an artist, by choice a writer, it seemed to him more than a little ridiculous that anyone should be under the necessity of earning a living. The death of a member of the lower orders could be trusted to give him a mild chuckle. I think this attitude was emphasised by the fact that, himself of good family, he could not have dwelt long in England without becoming aware that to the English one American was very like another. He saw compatriots on the strength of a fortune acquired in Michigan or Ohio received with as great cordiality as though they belonged to the eminent families of Boston and New York, and in self-defence somewhat exaggerated his native fastidiousness in social relations. Sometimes he made rather ludicrous mistakes and would attribute to some young man who had taken his fancy a distinction which he obviously did not possess.

If in these pages I have made Henry James, I hope not unkindly, a trifle absurd it is because that is what I found him. I think he took himself a good deal too seriously. We look askance at a man who keeps on telling you he is a gentleman; I think it would have been more becoming in Henry James if he had not insisted so often on his being an artist. It is better to leave others to say that. But he was gracious, hospitable and when in the mood uncommonly amusing. He had uncommon gifts and if I think they were too often ill-directed that is only what I think and I ask no one to agree with me. The fact remains that those last novels of his, notwithstanding their unreality, make all other novels, except the very best, unreadable.

III

I met H. G. Wells for the first time at a flat which Reggie Turner had near Berkeley Square. I was living then in Mount Street and sometimes I would drop in to see him. Reggie Turner was on the whole the most amusing man I have known. I will not attempt to describe his humour, since Max Beerbohm has done it to perfection in the essay called *Laughter*. Reggie was not so well pleased as he might have been with this flattering tribute because Max had added that he was not very responsive to the humour of others. He asked me if it was true, and I was bound to admit that it was. Reggie liked an audience, though he was quite content with one of three or four, and then he would take a theme and embroider upon it with such drollery that he made your sides so ache with laughter that at last you had to beg him to stop. He was by way of being a novelist, but somehow, when he took up his pen his gaiety, his extravagant invention, his lightness deserted him, and his novels were dull. They were unsuccessful. He said of them: 'With most novelists it's their first edition that is valuable, but with mine it's the second. It doesn't exist.' I will set down here a quip of his because I do not think it is well known. He was one of the few of Oscar Wilde's friends who remained faithful to him after his disgrace. Reggie was in Paris when Wilde, living in a cheap, dingy hotel on the left bank of the Seine, was dying. Reggie went to see him every day. One morning he found him distraught. He asked him what was the matter. 'I had a terrible dream last night,' said Oscar, 'I dreamt I was supping with the dead.' 'Well,' said Reggie, 'I'm sure you were the life and soul of the party, Oscar.' Wilde burst into a roar of laughter and regained his spirits. It was not only witty, but kind.

On the day on which I was first introduced to H. G. he had been lunching with Reggie and they had gone back to his flat to continue their conversation. H. G. was then, I suppose, at the height of his fame. I had not expected to find him there and was slightly disconcerted. I had recently made a success as a dramatist which the newspapers described as spectacular, but I was well aware that I had thereby lost caste with the intelligentsia. H. G. was cordial enough, but, perhaps because I was sensitive, I received the impression that he looked upon me with a sort of off-hand amusement as he might have looked upon Arthur Roberts or Dan Leno. He was busy reconstructing the world according to his own notions of how it should be shaped, and he had no time for anyone who was not with him, so that he could be enlisted to serve his ideas, or against him, so that he could be reasoned with, argued with, and if not brought round ignominiously discarded.

Though after that I saw him now and then, it was not till a number of years later, when I had settled down on the Riviera and H. G. had a house there too at which he spent a considerable part of the year, that our slight acquaintance ripened into friendship. Later still, when he had parted with the companion who shared the house with him (carved on the chimney-piece in the sitting-room was the phrase: This house was built by two lovers), and abandoned it to her, he would from time to time come to stay with me. He was very good company. He was not a wit as Max Beerbohm or Reggie Turner was, but he had a lively sense of humour and could laugh at himself as well as at others. Once he asked me to lunch to meet Barbusse, the author of a novel called *Le Feu* that had made a great stir. It is a long time ago and I can only remember that Barbusse was a long, thin, hirsute man dressed in shabby black like a mute at a French funeral. He had dark angry eyes and a restless manner. He was an ardent, violent socialist and his speech was torrential. Though H. G. understood French well enough he spoke it haltingly, so that Barbusse had the conversation pretty much to himself. He treated us as though we were a public meeting. When he left, H. G. turned to me with a wry smile and said: 'How silly our own ideas sound when we hear them out of somebody else's mouth.' He was sharp-witted and, though apt to find persons who didn't agree with him stupid and so objects of ridicule, the humour he exercised at their expense was devoid of malice.

H. G. had strong sexual instincts and he said to me more than once that the need to satisfy these instincts had nothing to do with love. It was a purely physiological matter. If humour, as some say, is incompatible with love, then H. G. was never in love, for he was keenly alive to what was rather absurd in the objects of his unstable affections and sometimes seemed almost to look upon them as creatures of farce. He was incapable of the idealisation of the desired person which most of us experience when we fall in love. If his companion was not intelligent he soon grew bored with her, and if she was her intelligence sooner or later palled on him. He did not like his cake unsweetened and if it was sweet it cloyed. He loved his liberty and when he found that a woman wished to restrict it he became exasperated and somewhat ruthlessly broke off the connection. Sometimes this was not so easily done and he had to put up with scenes and recriminations that even he found difficult to treat with levity. He was of course like most creative persons self-centred. That to sever a tie that had lasted for years might cause the other party pain and humiliation appeared to him merely silly. I was somewhat closely concerned in one of these upheavals in his life, and speaking of the trouble it was causing him he said: 'You know, women often mistake possessiveness for passion and when they are left, it is not so much that their heart is broken as that their claim to property is repudiated.' He thought it unreasonable that what on his side was merely the relaxation from what he regarded as his life's work on the other might be enduring passion. This he aroused. It surprised me since his physical appearance was not particularly pleasing. He was fat and homely. I once asked one of his mistresses what especially attracted her in him. I expected her to say his acute mind and his sense of fun; not at all; she said that his body smelt of honey.

Notwithstanding H. G.'s immense reputation and the great influence he had had on his contemporaries he was devoid of conceit. There was nothing of the stuffed shirt in him. He never put on airs. He had naturally good manners and he would treat some unknown scribbler, the assistant librarian, for instance, of a provincial library, with the same charming civility as if he were as important as himself. It was only later that by a grin and a quip you could tell what a donkey he had thought him. I remember attending a dinner of the P.E.N., of which H. G. was then president. There were a great many people present and after H. G. had read a report a number of them got up to ask questions. Most of them were silly, but H. G. replied to them all with great courtesy. One thickly bearded man, which marked him out as a conscious intellectual, leapt to his feet time and again to make short speeches of a singular ineptitude and it was only too obvious that he was trying merely to attract attention to himself. H. G. could have crushed him with a retort, but he listened to him attentively and then reasoned with him as if he had been talking sense. After the proceedings were over I told

H. G. how much I admired the wonderful patience with which he had dealt with the silly fellow. He chuckled and said: 'When I was a member of the Fabian Society I got a lot of practice in dealing with fools.'

He had no illusions about himself as an author. He always insisted that he made no pretension to be an artist. That was, indeed, something he despised rather than admired, and when he spoke of Henry James, an old friend, who claimed, as I have hinted, perhaps a little too often that he was an artist and nothing else, it was good-humouredly to ridicule him. 'I'm not an author,' H. G. would say, 'I'm a publicist. My work is just high-class journalism.' On one occasion, after he had been staying with me, he sent me a complete edition of his works and next time he came he saw them displayed in an imposing row on my shelves. They were well printed on good paper and handsomely bound in red. He ran his finger along them and with a cheerful grin said: 'They're as dead as mutton, you know. They all dealt with matters of topical interest and now that the matters aren't topical any more they're unreadable.' There is a good deal of truth in what he said. He had a fluent pen and too often it ran away with him. I have never seen any of his manuscripts, but I surmise that he wrote with facility and corrected little. He had a way of repeating in one sentence, but in other words, exactly what he said in the previous one. I suppose it was because he was so full of the idea he wanted to express that he was not satisfied to say it only once. It made him unnecessarily verbose.

H. G.'s theory of the short story was a sensible one. It enabled him to write a number that were very good and several that were masterly. His theory of the novel was different. His early novels, which he had written to earn a living, did not accord with it and he spoke of them slightingly. His notion was that the function of the novelist was to deal with the pressing problems of the day and to persuade the reader to adopt the views

177

for the betterment of the world which he, H. G., held. He was fond of likening the novel to a woven tapestry of varied interest, and he would not accept my objection that after all a tapestry has unity. The artist who designed it has given it form, balance, coherence and arrangement. It is not a jumble of unrelated items.

His later novels are, if not, as he said, unreadable, at least difficult to read with delight. You begin to read them with interest, but as you go on you find your interest dwindle and it is only by an effort of will that you continue to read. I think *Tono Bungay* is generally considered his best novel. It is written with his usual liveliness, though perhaps the style is better suited to a treatise than to a novel, and the characters are well presented. He has deliberately avoided the suspense which most novelists attempt to create and he tells you more or less early on what is going to happen. His theory of the novelist's function allows him to digress abundantly, which, if you are interested in the characters and their behaviour, can hardly fail to arouse in you some impatience.

One day when he was staying with me in the course of conversation he made the remark: 'Im only interested in people in the mass, I'm indifferent to the individual.' Then with a smile: 'I like you, in fact I've got a real affection for you, but I'm not interested in you.' I laughed. I knew it was true. 'I'm afraid I can't multiply myself by ten thousand to arouse your interest, old boy,' I said. 'Ten thousand?' he cried. 'That's nothing. Ten million.' During the course of his life he came in contact with a great many people, but with rare exceptions, though consistently pleasant and courteous, they made no more impression on him than the 'extras' who compose the crowd in a moving picture.

I think that is why his novels are less satisfactory than one would have liked them to be. The people he puts before you are not individuals, but lively and talkative marionettes whose function it is to express the ideas he was out to attack or to defend. They do not develop according to their dispositions, but change for the purposes of the theme. It is as though a tadpole did not become a frog, but a squirrel – because you had a cage that you wanted to pop him into. H. G. seems often to have grown tired of his characters before he was half-way through and then, frankly discarding any attempt at characterisation, he becomes an out-and-out pamphleteer. One curious thing that you can hardly help noticing if you have read most of H. G.'s novels is that he deals with very much the same people in book after book. He appears to have been content to use with little variation the few persons who had played an intimate part in his own life. He was always a little impatient with his heroines. He regarded his heroes with greater indulgence. He had of course put more of himself in them; most of them in fact are merely himself in a different guise. Trafford in *Marriage* is indeed the portrait of the man H. G. thought he was, added to the man he would have liked to be.

IV

In the last twenty-five years I have had a lot of people staying with me, and sometimes I am tempted to write an essay on guests. There are the guests who never shut a door after them and never turn out the light when they leave their room. There are the guests who throw themselves on their bed in muddy boots to have a nap after lunch, so that the counterpane has to be cleaned on their departure. There are the guests who smoke in bed and burn holes in your sheets. There are the guests who are on a régime and have to have special food cooked for them and there are the guests who wait till their glass is filled with a vintage claret and then say: 'I won't have any, thank you.' There are the guests who never put back a book in the place from which they took it and there are the guests who take away a volume from a set and never return it. There are the guests who borrow money from you when they are leaving and do not pay it back. There are the guests who can never be alone for a minute and there are the guests who are seized with a desire to talk the moment they see you glancing at a paper. There are the guests who, wherever they are, want to be somewhere else and there are the guests who want to be doing something from the time they get up in the morning till the time they go to bed at night. There are the guests who treat you as though they were gauleiters in a conquered province. There are the guests who bring three weeks laundry with them to have washed at your expense and there are the guests who send their clothes to the cleaners and leave you to pay the bill. There are the guests who take all they can get and offer nothing in return.

There are also the guests who are happy just to be with you, who seek to please, who have resources of their own, who amuse you, whose conversation is delightful, whose interests are varied, who exhilarate and excite you, who in short give you far more than you can ever hope to give them and whose visits are only too brief. Such a guest was H. G. He had a social sense. When there was a party he wanted to make it go. Now and then there were neighbours who had to be asked to lunch or dine and sometimes they were dull. H. G. would talk to them as entertainingly as if they had the wits to understand him. One such occasion stands out in my memory because it is the only time I saw him defeated. One of my neighbours, hearing that he was staying with me, called me up and told me that she had a great admiration for him and that she'd always been told that he was a marvellous talker and would so much like to meet him. I asked her to lunch. We sat down and H. G., who liked to talk, began to do so. He had just got into his stride when the lady interrupted him with a remark which showed that she hadn't listened to a word he said. He stopped, and when she had finished went on. Again she interrupted him and again he stopped. When she paused he started once more and again she interrupted. It was evident that her wish was not to hear H. G. talk, but to have him listen to her talk. He gave me one of his funny grins and relapsed into silence. For the rest of lunch he sat mute while she cheerfully gave utterance to a stream of shattering platitudes. When she went away she said she'd had a wonderful time.

I saw H. G. for the last time during the war. I was in New York and he had come to America to deliver a series of lectures. He came to lunch with me just before his return to England. He looked old, tired and shrivelled. He was as perky as ever, but with something of an effort. His lectures were a dismal failure. He was not a good speaker. It was odd that after so much public speaking he had never been able to deliver a discourse, but was obliged to read it. His voice was thin and squeaky and he read with his nose in his manuscript. People couldn't hear what he said and they left in droves. He had also seen a number of highly influential persons, but though they listened to him politely he could not but see that they paid little attention to what he said. He was hurt and disappointed. 'I've been saying the same things to people for the last thirty years,' he said to me with exasperation, 'and they won't listen.' That was the trouble. He had said the same things too often. Many of his ideas were sensible, none of them was complicated; but, like Goethe, he thought that one must always repeat truth: *Man muss das Wahre immer wiederholen.* He was so constituted that never a doubt entered his mind that he was definitely possessed of *das Wahre.* Naturally people grew impatient when they were asked once more to listen to views they knew only too well. He had had an immense influence on a whole generation and had done a great deal to alter the climate of opinion. But he had had his say. He was mortified to find that people looked upon him as a has-been. They agreed with him or they didn't. When they listened to him it was no longer with the old thrill of excitement, but with the indulgence you accord to an old man who has outlived his interest.

He died a disappointed man.

V

H. G. set little store on the pure novelist. I think he would have segregated the novelists who seek primarily to entertain on an island next to the one on which in *A New Utopia* he settled the drunkards, where, well-fed and comfortably housed, they could spend their leisure in reading one another's works. The only straight novelist with whom he was on terms of real intimacy was Arnold Bennett. A woman I knew told me how once standing next to Henry James at a very grand party at Londonderry House, one of those parties graced by royalty, where decorations were worn, stars and impressive ribbons, and the women blazed with diamonds, she had perhaps flippantly said to him: 'Fun, isn't it, for middle-class people like you and me to find ourselves hobnobbing with all these swells.' She saw at once by the look on his face that she had said the wrong thing. He didn't at all like being called middle class, and the look of amusement in her eyes when she noticed his annoyance increased his displeasure. Henry James was wrong to take offence, for after all it is the middle class that has created the wealth of English literature. That is natural enough. The boy of poor parents has received a scanty education and is forced to go to work at an early age. He has had little opportunity to read. The boy born in the upper ranks of society is seduced by the amusements his circumstances put within his easy reach, and his ambition, if he has any, is more likely to lead him to seek distinction in the way approved of by the people among whom his happy lot is cast. In either case his urge to create must be very strong to overcome the hindrances, though very different in character, which combine to thwart him. The nobility and gentry, so far as I know, have only produced two poets whose work is definitely a part of English literature, Shelley and Byron, and only one novelist, Fielding. The youth of middle-class parentage who has an irresistible impulse to write has received an education which is at least adequate; he has had access to something of a library; he has probably come in contact with a greater variety of people than either the son of an artisan or the son of a country squire; and though his family may deplore his taking to the hazardous profession of literature the idea is not quite foreign to their prepossessions and may even make a certain appeal to their pride. The English middle class is never without the desire to rise in the social scale and to have a writer in the family is to the clergyman, the solicitor, the Civil Servant something of a prestige item.

I think H. G. and Arnold were drawn together because both were of modest origin and both had had an arduous struggle to win recognition. After they had achieved success both felt that, though for somewhat different reasons, they stood slightly apart from the rest of the literary world, and that again was a bond between them. But the chief cause of H. G.'s genuine attachment to Arnold was that Arnold was a very lovable man.

I first knew him in 1904 when we were both living in Paris. I had taken a tiny apartment near the Lion de Belfort, on the fifth floor, from which I had a spacious view of the cemetery of Montparnasse. I used to dine at a restaurant in the rue d'Odessa. A number of painters, illustrators, sculptors and writers were in the habit of dining there and we had a little room to ourselves. We got a very good dinner, *vin compris*, for two francs fifty, and it was usual to give four sous to Marie, the good-humoured and sharp-tongued maid who waited on us. We were of various nationalities and the conversation was carried on indifferently in English and French. On occasion someone would bring his mistress and her mother, whom he introduced politely to the company as *ma belle mère*, but for the most part we were all men. We discussed every subject under the sun, generally with heat, and by the time we came to coffee (with which, I seem to remember, a *fine* was thrown in) and lit our cigars, *demi londrès* at three sous apiece, the air was heady. We differed with extreme acrimony. Arnold used to come there once a week. He reminded me years later that the first time we met, which was at this restaurant, I was white with passion. The conversation was upon the merits of Hérédia. I asserted that there was no sense in him, and a painter scornfully replied that you didn't want sense in poetry, you wanted sound. Someone contributed an anecdote about Mallarmé and Degas. Degas arrived late at one of Mallarmé's celebrated Tuesdays and said he'd been trying all day to write a sonnet and couldn't get an idea. To this Mallarmé replied: 'But, my dear Degas, one doesn't write a sonnet with ideas, one writes it with words.' From this an argument arose upon the objects and limitations of poetry which soon enlivened the whole company. I exercised such powers as I had of sarcasm, invective and vituperation, and my antagonist, Roderic O'Connor by name, a taciturn Irishman, than whom there is no man more difficult to cope with, was coldly and bitingly virulent. The entire table took up the dispute and I have still a dim recollection of Arnold, smiling a little, calm and a trifle Olympian, putting in now and then a brief, dogmatic, but, I am certain, judicious remark. He was older than most of us. He was then a thin man, with dark hair very smoothly done in a fashion that suggested the private soldier of the day. He was much more neatly dressed than we were and more conventionally. He looked like a managing clerk in a city office. At that time the only book he had written that we knew of was *The Grand Babylon Hotel* and our attitude towards him was somewhat patronising. We were arrogantly high-brow. Some of us had read the book and enjoyed it, which was enough for us to decide that there was nothing in it, but the rest shrugged their shoulders and declined to waste their time over such trash. Had you read *Marie Donadieu*? That was the stuff to give the troops.

Arnold was living at that time in Montmartre, I think in the Rue de Calais, in a small dark apartment which he had filled with Empire furniture. It was certainly not genuine, but this he did not know, and he was exceedingly proud of it. Arnold was a tidy man and his apartment was very neat, with every article in an appointed place, but it was not very comfortable and you could not imagine anyone making a home of it. It gave you the impression of a 'set' arranged for a man who saw himself in a certain rôle which he was playing conscientiously, but into the skin of which he hadn't quite got. On deciding to live in Paris Arnold had given up the editorship of a magazine called *Woman* and was settled down to train himself for the profession of literature. Through Marcel Schwob he had got to know several of the French writers of the day, and I seem to remember his telling me that Schwob had taken him to see Anatole France, who was then the high priest of French letters. Arnold diligently read the French literary reviews, of which at that time the *Mercure de France* was the most distinguished; he read Stendhal and Flaubert, but chiefly Balzac, and I think he told me that he had read through the whole of the *Comédie Humaine* in a year. When I first knew him he was starting on the Russians and talked with enthusiasm of *Anna Karenina*. He thought it the greatest of all novels. I am under the impression that he did not discover Chekov till somewhat later. When he did, he began to admire Tolstoi less.

Arnold's plan of campaign to achieve success in his

calling was cut-and-dried. He proposed to make his annual expenditure by writing novels, and by writing plays to make provision for his old age. He meant to write two or three books to get his hand in and then write a masterpiece. When I asked him what sort of book this was going to be he said, something on the lines of *A Great Man;* but that, he added, had brought him in nothing at all and he couldn't afford to go on in that style till he was properly established. I listened, but attached no importance to what he said. I did not think him capable of writing anything of consequence. Because I had lately had my first play produced by the Stage Society he asked me to read one of his. The characters were plausible and the dialogue natural, but in his determination to be realistic he had allowed none of them to make a witty or even a clever remark and had, so it seemed to me, gone out of his way to eschew anything in the nature of dramatic action. As a picture of middle-class life the play had verisimilitude, but I found it dull. Perhaps only it was before its time.

Like everyone else who lives in Paris Arnold had come across a particular little restaurant where you could get a better dinner for less money than anywhere else. This one was on the first floor, somewhere in Montmartre, and now and then I used to go over to dine, Dutch Treat, with him. After dinner we went back to his apartment and he would play Beethoven on a cottage piano. He was nothing if not thorough, and it was obvious that if you were living in Montmartre as a man of letters and a Bohemian (though a clean, respectable one) to complete the picture you must have a mistress. But that costs money and Arnold, who had come to Paris for a definite purpose and had only a certain sum to dispose of, was too cagey to squander on luxuries what he needed for necessities. He was not a son of the Five Towns for nothing and he solved the problem in a characteristic fashion. One night after we had been dining together and were sitting amid the Empire furniture of his apartment, he said:

'Look here, I have a proposal to make to you.'

'Oh?'

'I have a mistress with whom I spend two nights a week. She has another gentleman with whom she spends two other nights. She likes to have her Sundays to herself and she's looking for someone who'll take the two nights she has free. I've told her about you. She likes writers. I'd like to see her nicely fixed up and I thought it would be a good plan if you took the two nights that she has vacant.'

The suggestion startled me.

'It sounds rather cold-blooded to me,' I said.

'She's not an ignorant woman, you know,' Arnold insisted. 'Not by any manner of means. She reads a great deal, Madame de Sévigné and all that, and she can talk very intelligently.'

But even that didn't tempt me.

Arnold was good company, and I always enjoyed spending an evening with him, but I didn't very much like him. He was cocksure and bumptious, and he was rather common. I don't say this depreciatingly, but as I might say that someone was short and fat. I left Paris after a year and so lost touch with him. He wrote one or two books which I did not read. The Stage Society produced a play of his which I liked. I wrote and told him so and he wrote to thank me and in the course of his letter laid out the critics who had not thought so well of the play as I had. I can't remember whether it was before or after this that *The Old Wives' Tale* was published. I began reading it with misgiving, but this quickly changed to astonishment. I had never supposed that Arnold could write anything so good. I was deeply impressed. I thought it a great book. I have read many appreciations of it, and I think everything has been said but one thing, which is that it is eminently readable. I should not mention a merit that is so obvious except that many great books do not possess it. It is the novelist's most precious gift, and it is one that Arnold had even in his slightest and most trivial pieces. I have of late read *The Old Wives' Tale* again. Though written in rather a drab style, with an occasional use of 'literatese' which gives you a jolt, and without elegance, it is still extremely readable. The characters ring true: they are not intrinsically interesting, it was not to Arnold's purpose to make them brilliant, and it is a mark of his skill that notwithstanding you follow their fortunes with interest and sympathy. Their motives are plausible and they behave as from what you know of them you would expect them to behave. The incidents are completely probable: Sophia is in Paris during the siege and the Commune; an author less determined to avoid the sensational would have looked upon it as an opportunity, by describing scenes of terror, anguish and bloodshed, to give his narrative a lift. Not Arnold. Sophia goes about her business unperturbed; she looks after her lodgers, buys and hoards food, makes money when she can, and in fact conducts herself precisely as of course the great mass of the people did.

The Old Wives' Tale was slow to make its way. I think I am right in saying that it was received favourably, but not with frantic eulogy, and that its circulation was inconsiderable. For a time it looked as though it would have no more than the sort of *succès d'estime* that *Maurice Guest* had and be forgotten as all but one novel out of a thousand is forgotten. By a happy chance, however, it was brought to the attention of George Doran, an American publisher, and he bought sheets; he then acquired the American rights, set it up and launched it on its triumphal course. It was not until after its great success in America that it was taken over by another publisher in England and won favour with the British public.

For many years, what with one thing and another, I do not think I met Arnold, or if I did it was only at a party, literary or otherwise, at which I had the opportunity to say no more than a few words to him; but after the First World War and until his death I saw him frequently. By this time he had become a 'character'. He was very different from the thin, rather insignificant man that I had known in Paris. He had grown stout. His hair, very grey, was worn long and he had cultivated the amusing cock's comb that the caricaturists made famous. He walked with an arrogant strut, his back arched and his head thrown back. He had always been neat in his dress, disconcertingly even, but now he was grand. He wore a fob and frilled shirts in the evening and took an immense pride in his white waistcoats. At one time he had a yacht and he dressed the part of the owner in style. Yachting cap, blue coat with brass buttons, white trousers: no actor playing the rôle in a musical comedy could have arrayed himself more perfectly in character. In one of his diaries he has related the story of a picnic I took him on while he was staying with me in the South of France. I had a motor-boat then and after picking up the rest of my guests in Cannes we went over to the Isle Sainte Marguerite to bathe, eat *bouillabaisse* and gossip. The women wore pyjamas and the men tennis shirts, ducks and espadrilles, but Arnold, refusing to permit himself such *sans gène*, was dressed in a check suit of a sort of mustard colour, fancy socks and fancy shoes, a striped shirt, a starched collar and a foulard tie. After lunch a violent mistral sprang up which prevented us from leaving the island. Some of the persons present took the prospect without amenity of being marooned for an indefinite period and when twelve hours later the sea had sufficiently calmed down to allow us to risk the crossing more than one of them faced the slight danger we were in with a good deal of anxiety. Arnold throughout remained dignified, self-possessed, good-tempered and interested. When at six in the morning, bedraggled and unshaven, we at last got home, he, in his smart shirt and neat suit, looked as dapper and well-groomed as he had looked eighteen hours before.

But it was not only in appearance that Arnold differed from the man I had known before. Life had changed him. I think it possible that when I first knew him he was hampered by a certain diffidence and his bumptiousness was assumed to conceal it. Success had given him confidence. It had certainly mellowed him. He had acquired a proper assurance of his own merit. He told me once that there were only two novels written during the first twenty years of the century that he was confident would survive and one of them was *The Old Wives' Tale.* It may be that he was right. That depends on the whirligig of taste. Realism is a fashion that comes and goes. When readers ask their novels to give them fantasy, romance, excitement, suspense, surprise, they will find Arnold's masterpiece pedestrian and rather dull. When the pendulum swings back and they want homely truth, verisimilitude, good sense and sympathetic delineation of character they will find it in *The Old Wives' Tale.*

I have said before that Arnold was a lovable man. His very oddities were endearing. Indeed it was to them that the great affection in which he was held was largely owing, for people laughed at foibles in him of which they believed themselves exempt and thus mitigated the oppression which his talent must otherwise have made them feel. They liked him all the better for the absurdities which gave them a comfortable sense of superiority. He was never what in England is technically known as a gentleman, but he was never vulgar any more than the traffic surging up Ludgate Hill is vulgar. He was devoid of envy. He was generous. He was courageous. He always said with perfect frankness what he thought and because it never struck him that he could offend he seldom did; but if, with his quick sensitiveness, he imagined that he had hurt somebody's feelings, he did everything in reason to salve the wound. But only in reason. If the affronted person continued to bear a grudge he dismissed him with a shrug of the shoulders and a 'silly ass'. He retained to the end an engaging naïvety. He was convinced that there were two things he knew all about – money and women. His friends were unanimous in agreeing that this was an illusion. It got him now and then into trouble. With all his common sense, and he had more common sense than most of us, he made the mistake to which many novelists are prone, of ordering his life after the pattern of one of the novels he might very well have written. In a work of fiction the author can pull the strings and with sufficient skill on the whole get his characters to act as he wants them to. In real life people are more difficult to cope with.

I was surprised to see how patronising in general were the obituary notices written at Arnold's death. A good deal of fun was made of his obsession with grandeur and luxury, and the pleasure he took in *trains de luxe* and first-class hotels. He never grew quite accustomed to the appurtenances of wealth. Once he said to me: 'If you've ever really been poor you remain poor at heart all your life. I've often walked,' he added, 'when I could very well afford to take a taxi because I simply couldn't bring myself to waste the shilling it would cost.' He admired and disapproved of extravagance.

The criticism to which he devoted much time during his later years came in for a good deal of adverse comment. He loved his position on the *Evening Standard*. He liked the power it gave him and enjoyed the interest his articles aroused. The immediate response, like the applause an actor receives after an effective scene, gratified his appetite for actuality. It gave him the illusion, peculiarly pleasant to the author whose avocation necessarily entails a sense of apartness, that he was in the midst of things. Whatever he thought, he said without fear or favour. He had no patience with the precious, the affected or the pompous. If he thought little of writers who are now more praised

191

than read it is not certain that he thought wrongly. He was more interested in life than in art. In criticism he was an amateur. The professional critic is probably somewhat shy of life, for otherwise it is unlikely that he will devote himself to the reading and judging of books rather than to the stress and turmoil of living. He is more at ease with it when the sweat has dried and the acrid odour of humanity has ceased to offend the nostrils. He can be sympathetic enough to the realism of Defoe and the tumultuous vitality of Balzac, but when it comes to the productions of his own day he feels more comfortable with works in which a deliberately literary attitude has softened the asperities of reality.

That is why, I suppose, the praise that was accorded to Arnold for *The Old Wives' Tale* after his death was cooler than one would have expected. Some of the critics said that notwithstanding everything he had a sense of beauty, and they quoted passages to show his poetic power and his feeling for the mystery of existence. I do not see the point of making out that he had something of what you would have liked him to have a great deal more of and ignoring that in which his power and value lay. He was neither mystic nor poet. He was interested in material things and in the humours of common men in general and he described life, as every writer does, in the terms of his own temperament.

Arnold was afflicted with a very bad stammer; it was painful to watch the struggle he sometimes had to get the words out. It was torture to him. Few realised the exhaustion it caused him to speak. What to most men is as easy as breathing was to him a constant strain. It tore his nerves to pieces. Few knew the humiliations it exposed him to, the ridicule it excited in many, the impatience it aroused, the awkwardness of feeling that it made people find him tiresome, the minor exasperation of thinking of a good, amusing or apt remark and not venturing to say it in case the stammer ruined it. Few knew the distressing sense it gave rise to of a bar to complete contact with other men. It may be that except for the stammer which forced him to introspection Arnold would never have become a writer. But I think it is no small proof of his strong and sane character that notwithstanding this impediment he was able to retain his splendid balance and regard the normal life of man from a normal point of view.

The Old Wives' Tale is certainly the best book he wrote. He never lost the desire to write another as good and because it was written by an effort of will he thought he could repeat it. He tried in *Clayhanger*, and for a time it looked as though he might succeed. I think he failed only because his material fizzled out. After *The Old Wives' Tale* he had not enough left to complete the vast structure he had designed. No writer can get more than a certain amount of ore out of one seam; when he has got that, though it remains, miraculously, as rich as before, it is only others who can profitably work it. Arnold tried again in *Lord Raingo*, and he tried for the last time in *Imperial Palace*. In this I think the subject was at fault. Because it profoundly interested him he thought it was of universal interest. He gathered his data systematically, but they were jotted down in note-books and not garnered (as were those of *The Old Wives' Tale*) unconsciously, and preserved, not in black and white, but as old memories in his bones, in his nerves, in his heart. But that Arnold should have spent the last of his energy and determination on the description of an hotel seems to me to have symbolic significance. For I feel that he was never quite at home in the world. It was to him perhaps a sumptuous hotel, with marble bathrooms and a perfect cuisine, in which he was a transient guest. I feel that he was, here among men, impressed, delighted, but a little afraid of doing the wrong thing and never entirely at his ease. Just as his little apartment in the rue de Calais years before had suggested to me a part played carefully, but from the outside, I feel that to him life was a rôle that he played conscientiously, and with ability, but into the skin of which he never quite got.

I remember that once, beating his knee with his clenched fist to force the words from his writhing lips, he said: 'I am a nice man.' He was.

VI

I mentioned early in this essay that I was introduced to Henry James by Elizabeth Russell. I knew her slightly over a number of years, but when she built herself a house near Mougins, which is an easy hour's drive from my own, I saw her fairly often, and so came to know her much better. She made her reputation with three books, starting with *Elizabeth and her German Garden*, when she was still Countess von Arnim, but later on wrote a number of novels in a style in which the English have never had much success. This is the light, amusing novel which is not an outrage to the intelligence. I think the English are apt to be suspicious of books that are so entertaining and so easy to read. Farce they wallow in, but high comedy causes them a vague discomfort. Perhaps it makes them feel that the author is poking fun at them. And it is true that Elizabeth was inclined to be flippant about matters that we are more inclined to take seriously. She was a little, rather plump woman, not pretty, but with a pleasant, open, frank face, which was a very fallacious indication of her character. In one of his aphorisms Pearsall Smith said: 'Hearts that are delicate and kind and tongues that are neither – these make the finest company in the world.' I do not know whether Elizabeth's heart, except where dogs were concerned, was delicate and kind, but her tongue was neither and she was very good company. She regarded her fellow-creatures with a robust common sense which some thought verged on the cynical. It was typical of her that over her writing-room she should have affixed the quotation: 'Peace, perfect peace, with loved ones far away.' She had a low voice and an innocent manner which added to the effect of the devastating things she said. She could be very malicious. I remember one occasion when I asked her to lunch because H. G., a very old friend of hers, was staying with me. He had recently published his autobiography and in the course of conversation he mentioned that he had gone down to see again the house, Up Park, where in his boyhood he had spent his holidays. His mother had been lady's maid to the owner and much later had returned as housekeeper. From time to time H. G. spent considerable periods there and as was natural enough lived, as the phrase goes, 'below stairs'.

'And this time, H. G.,' asked Elizabeth with her most ingenuous air, 'did you go in by the front door?'

It was said of course to embarrass him and for a moment succeeded. He flushed a little, grinned and did not answer. Afterwards another of my guests asked Elizabeth why she had put that awkward question to him. She opened her eyes wide and with a wonderful assumption of innocence answered: 'I wanted to know.'

I asked Elizabeth once whether the story I had often heard was true that when her husband was very ill she read to him as he lay in bed the book in which she had drawn a caustic portrait of him. When she reached the last page, so the story ran, shattered by what he had been made to listen to, he turned his face to the wall and died. She looked at me blandly and said:

'He was very ill. He would have died in any case.'

Elizabeth lived to a ripe old age and retained to the end the complacent air of a woman who knows she is attractive to men. Before I leave her I will recount a story she told which is not only characteristic, but so diverting that I think it would be a pity if it were forgotten. I don't know whether she told it to anybody else. She was living with her second husband, Lord Russell, on Telegraph Hill. When she went into the kitchen one morning she found the cook gasping; she asked what was the matter, and the cook told her that she had just cut off the head of the chicken they were to have for dinner that night, and then the headless chicken had laid an egg.

'Show it me,' said Elizabeth.

She looked at it pensively for a moment and then said:

'Give it to his lordship for breakfast tomorrow.'

Next morning, sitting at table opposite her husband, she watched him as he ate the boiled egg. When he had finished she asked him:

'Did you notice anything funny about that egg, Frank?'

'No,' he answered. 'Was there anything peculiar about it?'

'No, nothing,' she said, 'except that it was laid by a dead hen.'

He gave her a startled look, sprang to the window and vomited. With a demure smile she added to me:

'And d'you know, I don't believe he ever really loved me after that.'

I will end this essay with an account of my one and only meeting with Mrs. Wharton. She was then a well-known and highly esteemed novelist. Her short stories are ingenious and well-contrived, and in *Ethan Frome* she wrote a remarkably able novel about the country folk of New England; but her main interests lay with the rich and fashionable people who lived on Fifth Avenue and had sumptuous palaces at Newport. She described a phase of American civilisation which has long since passed away, and the manners and customs of her characters, their attitude towards the problems and difficulties that confront them, are so different from those of today that we can only believe what she tells us because we know that she wrote of what she knew. Her novels have now the same sort of charm that time gives to certain pictures regardless of their artistic merit. The crinolines, the bustles that women wore, as fashion changed made them absurd, but today, with the passing of the years, they have become 'costume' and give us an amused delight. Mrs. Wharton's style was easy, pleasant and not undistinguished. She deserves a place, even though but a minor one, in American literature.

Mrs. Wharton lived in Paris, but sometimes came to England, chiefly, I think, to see Henry James, who was an intimate and revered friend; and on these visits she spent a few days in London. On one of these occasions Lady St. Helier asked her to lunch and asked me too. She had a large house in Portland Place and she entertained a great deal. People were inclined to laugh at her because she was something of a lion-hunter, but they accepted her invitations with alacrity since they were pretty sure to find themselves in company with persons who were either eminent, amusing or notorious. When a certain man was being tried for what looked like a peculiarly callous murder and his birth and antecedents made the case the talk of high society one bright young spark asked another if he knew the accused. 'No,' he answered, 'but if he isn't hanged I shall certainly meet him at Lady St. Helier's next week.' The party to which I was bidden was choice and rather select, and because besides Mrs. Wharton I was the only author present, when lunch was over my hostess took me up to her so that we could have a chat. She was seated in the middle of a small French sofa in such a way as to give it the appearance of a throne, and since she gave no indication that she wished to share it with me I took a chair and sat down in front of her. She was a smallish woman, with fine eyes, regular features and a pale clear skin drawn rather tightly over the bones of her face. She was dressed with the sober magnificence suitable to a woman of birth, of wealth and of letters. She made the other ladies there, all of exalted rank, look dowdy and provincial. She talked and I listened. She talked very well. She talked for twenty minutes. In that time, with a light touch and well-chosen words, she traversed the fields of painting, music and literature. Nothing she said was commonplace, everything she said was just. She said exactly the right things about Maurice Barrès, André Gide and Paul Valéry; it was impossible not to concur with her admirable remarks upon Debussy and Stravinsky; and of course what she had to say about Rodin and Maioll, about Cézanne, Degas and Renoir was just what one would have wished her to say. I have never met anyone whose perceptions were so sensitive, whose opinions so sound and whose artistic sentiments so exemplary.

Though my literary friends do not, I am sorry to say, look upon me as a member of the intelligentsia, I very much enjoy the conversation of cultured persons and I think (perhaps mistakenly) that I can adequately hold my own with them. Indeed sometimes I gently lead them down the garden path of mysticism and when I talk to them of Denis the Areopagite and Fray Luis de Leon, throwing in Samkaracharia for good measure, I often have them gasping for breath like speckled trout on a river bank. But Mrs. Wharton got me down. Most people have a blind spot; many suffer from vagaries of taste. I was once sitting at the opera behind a distinguished and talented woman. The opera was *Tristan and Isolde*. At the end of the second act she gathered her ermine cloak around her shoulders and, turning to her companion, said: 'Let's go. There's not enough action in this play.' Of course she was right, but perhaps that wasn't quite the point. There are persons of intelligence and susceptibility who prefer Verdi to Wagner, Charlotte Brontë to Jane Austen and cold mutton to cold grouse. Mrs. Wharton was devoid of frailty. Her taste was faultless. She admired only what was admirable. But such is the frowardness of human nature (of mine at all events), in the end I began to grow a trifle restive. It would have been a comfort to me if I could have found a chink in the shining armour of her impeccable refinement, if she had unaccountably expressed a sneaking tenderness for something that was downright vulgar; if, for instance, she had admitted to a secret passion for Marie Lloyd, or, though it had not yet burst on an enraptured world, had confided in me that she went to the Victoria Palace every night to hear *The Lambeth Walk*. But no. She said nothing but the right thing about the right person. The worst of it was that I could not but agree with everything she said. I could not bring myself to affirm that I thought Maioll boring and André Gide silly. She said about everyone that she so lightly touched upon, for there was nothing pedantic in her discourse, precisely what I thought myself and what every right-minded person should think. I cannot imagine anything more exasperating.

At last I said to her: 'And what do you think of Edgar Wallace?'

'Who is Edgar Wallace?' she replied.

'Do you never read thrillers?' I asked.

'No.'

Never has a monosyllable contained more frigid displeasure, more shocked disapproval nor more wounded surprise. I will not say she blenched, for she was a woman of the world and she knew instinctively how to deal with a solecism, but her eyes wandered away and a little forced smile slightly curled her lips. The moment was embarrassing for both of us. Her manner was that of a woman to whom a man has made proposals offensive to her modesty, but which her good breeding tells her it will be more dignified to ignore than to make a scene about.

'I'm afraid it's getting very late,' said Mrs. Wharton.

I knew that my audience was at an end. I never saw her again. She was an admirable creature, but not my cup of tea.